TRIAGE

B. A. PAUL

*For Bryan: The not-so-young and slightly balding Realtor
from Straughn, Indiana
As promised: One smooth character, a steak dinner, and no
royalties*

PROLOGUE

Eight Years Ago
New York City

Shattered glass fell from the gurney mattress, crunching under the stretcher's wheels and skidding across the hot asphalt. The sliding doors of Mount Lombard Medical whooshed open, greeting the sweaty first responders with a burst of cold air. Trauma docs rushed into the ambulance bay and were smothered with humidity only New York City in August could muster.

The young EMT's dark skin glistened with perspiration as she began the rundown, her voice barely audible above the din. "Twenty-nine-year-old male, head-on MVA, two dead on scene. One was his wife. Another, a male passenger, unknown relation. Blood pressure—"

Craig blocked out all other input. Distant sirens, road-rager's car horns, and the wafting of helicopter blades. The shouting of the charge nurse. All noise but the beating of his heart in his ears muted into the background. Welcoming the adrenaline surge coursing through his body, Craig honed in on the lead EMT's rundown of the patient's vitals and bullet-point list of injuries: Major blood loss. Crushed tibia, open fractures. Thready pulse.

Unresponsive.

Craig's heartbeat slowed almost instantly, the internal rush ground to a halt.

This man wasn't going to make it. If, by some miracle, the man did live, he'd never be the same. Wife dead. Possibly a second family member, too. Or friend. Or coworker— whoever was in the car that didn't make it. And, given that "miracle," the man in front of him would wish he'd also died at the scene. Craig had seen it time and again. The turmoil that comes from accepting the reality of living with such traumatizing injuries.

He took a deep breath and pushed forward. This was Mount Lombard Medical, the trauma center with the best miracle-to-patient ratio ever. Craig and his team would spend the next two hours, maybe more, trying to save the man's life. In other words, trying to perform a miracle.

A second EMT team wrestling a gurney carrying an equally bloody, equally unresponsive patient rushed by Craig, and he directed his team to trauma bay one. He glanced back long enough to be sure someone qualified took charge of the female patient, the driver who'd plowed into the man lying supine in front of him.

Someone more than qualified did. His Emma.

She gave him "the look" as she listened to the EMT give report. His heart went from steady to sinking fast. Emma, in all her experience, knew her patient wouldn't make it, either.

It was going to be a Pillow-Talk Therapy night that

would end with them wrapped in each other's arms, rehashing their cases, nursing a bottle of wine, while Toby, their black lab pup, chased squirrels in his sleep at their feet.

They'd talk about miracles and how one didn't come to the crash victims at Mount Lombard that day.

They'd speak of what they wanted from their lives. The adrenaline rush of working Trauma six days a week? They loved it, especially on those miraculous occasions or on those days when they saved more than they lost. But could they do this forever? Could they keep up this kind of pace and start a family?

They'd dream of a new kind of life.

Then Emma and Craig Thompson would sleep off their stress, shower, eat a protein-packed breakfast, and swipe their entry badges bright and early the next morning at Mount Lombard.

The lanky gal from registration came bursting into the ER and shouted through trauma bay one's pulled curtain. "We've got another multiple coming in. Crash on the George Washington has Greenwood Trauma slammed."

"And we're about to be. All hands on deck, people!" Gone was the previous moment's thought that he'd work on the car crash victim until they were all satisfied the man wasn't savable. Part of trauma triage is knowing when to move on, and sometimes the impossible cases had to take a backseat to hope.

Craig passed instructions for his MVA to the charge nurse, who would page another trauma doctor to take Craig's place.

Emma did the same with a capable resident in bay four for her unlucky lady.

Another pair of ambulances was incoming in ninety seconds, each transporting burn victims from a house fire.

Craig's adrenaline dripped into his bloodstream afresh, slowly increasing his heart rate again.

Two minors. Kids always took precedence over the dead-before-they-got-here patients. At least when Craig was in charge.

Adrenaline rushing once again in full force, his feet were out the ambulance bay doors where he paced, waiting for the arrival of the first little girl. Emma did the same, her cheeks flushed in anticipation. In choreographed lock-step rhythm, the pair of trauma doctors paced toward and away from each other as they awaited their next challenges, fingers brushing slightly on each pass, eyes locking in knowing anticipation.

Until the screech of the sirens became ear-shattering and the race against the clock began all over again.

1

Present Day
Indianapolis, Indiana

CRAIG THOMPSON PARKED his Jeep behind the small strip mall in his usual spot and rolled up the windows. Despite the chilly November morning, Craig allowed Toby to hang ten all the way from their suburb bungalow, the dog slobbering down the passenger side door the entire trip. The usual crisp outline of the Indianapolis skyline was muted in fog, and Craig felt a pang of longing as he imagined what might be happening closer to the heart of things. The bustle of folks arriving at their jobs. The police on duty. Utility workers setting up orange cones, honking off commuters. The EMTs making runs. The trauma center and the emergency rooms, never sleeping, zinging with life-saving tasks all around the city...

But here, in the recently developed community of Bella Square, that big city bustle was a painted-on backdrop.

Of course, one could still hear the sirens and bustle of city life, even on the outskirts, but compared to the center of it all, it was... muted.

Craig slid the keycard into the lock on the back door to the salon nestled in a four-unit business complex and allowed Toby off his leash into the building. No crazy barking from the realty office next door meant Brian hadn't yet made it in with his inherited German shepherd. Toby's presence sent the shepherd into loud disapproval most mornings, making Craig glad there was an empty unit on the other side of Wagz. The space on the end held Hear-Clear. If the racket Wagz clients and Brian's Hackett made bothered the hard-of-hearing clients, Clarence, the audiologist, certainly never complained.

Craig flipped the light, dropped his satchel, and took off his baseball cap. He ran a hand through his wavy black hair and replaced the cap as Toby bounced around his legs. The dog was always happy to "go work."

"Settle, boy."

The nine-year-old black lab took his leave, all legs and flopping ears as he clacked and clicked toenails against the tile floor, heading for the water dish—more like a water trough—and settled onto a much-too-expensive orthopedic dog bed. Not that the dog needed orthopedic help yet; the bed was heavy enough that Toby wasn't as likely to drag it from room to room while Craig tried to work. For a pooch nearing the top end of the breed's lifespan, Toby was starting to show gray around his muzzle and beneath those knowing eyes, but his strength was still at its peak.

"Good, Toby."

Craig sighed, kissed his index finger, and placed it against the silver frame near the light switch. Emma in her wedding gown, arms wrapped around a ten-month-old

Toby. The puppy's tongue lolled out to one side, that dorky smile slid up half his face. Emma's long veil draped Toby's ebony body.

He pulled himself from Emma's bright smile and turned to the grooming station. The walls of Wagz were bright turquoise, Emma's favorite color. Craig had painted giant white circles all over, hoping beyond hope that they'd look like bubbles. He could suture the deepest wounds and crack ribs to restart a heart, but bubble art was beyond him. So, he printed off canine clip art and traced black outlines of long-haired spaniels and pudgy pugs inside the makeshift bubbles. People liked the whimsy, he supposed.

Craig pulled on his full-body waterproof apron and readied his supplies for the first customer, Max, a jubilant Golden retriever. Wagz had one big wash station and a couple of grooming tables. A few wire kennels lined the walls for dogs waiting their turn for a bath, cut, and fluff. A wall separated the grooming stations from the front entry.

Craig laid out extra towels on the counter; he always ended up with more suds on him than the dog did because Max couldn't stop wagging his tail through his entire spa day. He could secure him in the bathtub rig, harnessing the dog's energy, but Craig didn't mind the workout and he didn't mind the extra dose of happy that was in such short supply these days.

Things were getting better, he told himself. Little by little, the life he'd built before became like the skyline—a permanent fixture, but slightly grayed out. Craig and Emma, both ER trauma docs, had become a power couple in Queens despite their rural Hoosier upbringing. Most employees at Mount Lombard had bets on when the Thompsons would run the entire hospital. Everyone else said they'd make beautiful babies if they could divorce themselves from the jobs they so loved and get busy with other things. Craig and Emma declared Toby was their one and only baby and dove happily into their careers—and each other.

Behind the scenes, though, they wanted nothing more than a child of their own. And they would have, except as the years ticked off, they realized they couldn't. Perhaps in vitro would do the trick? If not, then adoption. For sure.

And when that time came, when a child would need more attention than their careers would allow, they'd open a grooming business. It was one of those pillow-talk therapy moments when the couple dreamed of something a little less taxing than trauma center life. Perhaps "Back Home Again in Indiana..."

Then they'd break out in bad harmony and finish the lyrics of the song, laughing through to the end.

"We could even have our own brand of finishing spray—all natural, of course."

"Of course." Anything for Emma. He remembered the feel of her in his arms as she rattled off flavors like Very Vanilla, Lavender Wiggles, and Uptown Hound—for the more distinguished clients. She was so different in his arms than in the ER—soft, vulnerable, whimsical. In the trauma center, she was a force to be reckoned with.

Until she wasn't.

Craig hadn't been able to stop the bleeding, then or now. He inhaled deeply, squared his shoulders, and pushed the nightmare that surfaced far too often back down in that space under his ribs where he stored it for safekeeping.

The door chime sounded, and happy woofs and whines escaped from Toby and Max as the dogs greeted and wrestled, Max's leash flopping loosely on the floor. Craig plastered on a smile and gave Duane an estimated pick-up time.

"Toby, settle."

Reluctantly, the lab returned to his bed, and Craig led Max to the tub and began the wash. On cue and as hoped, the tail-wagging drenched him in frothy suds. The door chimed again, and Craig was forced to leash Max to the harness.

"Don't do anything I wouldn't do, buddy." He gave the dog a head scratch. Craig wasn't expecting another customer so early and was hoping to have a light day.

"Be right there." He dried off his hands and stepped into the check-in area to find a woman with her back turned to him, looking out to the street.

"Ma'am? Can I help you?"

When she turned, Craig took a step back.

Melody Atkins. The "let's just be friends" woman he'd nearly given a shiny diamond to, but then Emma Cade caught his heart.

"Hi, Craig."

Melody, looking as startled as he felt, hugged a manila file folder closer to her chest and shifted her weight. He waited for a long moment before she went on. "Sorry, I—" She brushed a shaky hand through her blonde bob and squared her shoulders.

Craig stood frozen to the floor, staring with his jaw hanging, dumbfounded—a foreign sensation for him. "Melody," he choked out. "Uh, hi. Uh—"

"How've you been?" Then she cringed. He knew the look. Well-meaning people often ask all the same questions of those who've suffered a great loss—often without realizing the conflict it stirs up. Craig had been a prominent ER trauma mastermind, with headhunters from multiple healthcare entities vying for his skills. Now he stood in front of her in a dripping wet black apron surrounded by cartoon drawings of dogs.

And badly drawn bubbles.

He shook his head to clear the barrage of confusion and sing-songed, "I'm good. I'm good." He held her gaze for a second and then offered a cautious, "You?"

She hesitated, then held out her folder to him. Perplexed, he crossed the small storefront and took the file from her. She smelled of fresh autumn air and lavender.

"I finished my degree." She sputtered. "A master's in human resources. Something to support me, do my job, and then go back to my little corner of the world. Nice and quiet." She offered a quick smile.

He and Melody had often discussed that nice and quiet had never been Craig's cup of tea—especially back in high school when the world was ripe for the picking.

"That's good. That's good." He opened the folder and flipped through the pages, but the words were nothing more than black scratch marks on the white paper. He cleared his throat and glanced back at her. "What am I looking at?"

It was her turn to clear her throat. "I started work at Blane Park four years ago, right after..." She didn't need to finish. *Right after Emma died* would have been the next words out of her mouth had she continued.

His eyes widened, then tried to see the words on the pages again, but nothing registered.

"I think it might be about Emma," she said.

He jerked his head up and focused hard on her face.

"Emma. And all the others."

2

CRAIG'S KNEES went weak when Emma's name came out of Melody's lips, sending a searing wave of anxiety through his core. Seeing Melody after all this time stirred up memories, though he couldn't quite label the emotion that came with it. Nostalgia? Maybe. Regret? No, not that one. Emma was the right choice and completely owned his heart.

Sadness? There was always an undercurrent of sadness in his life, so who knows. Craig had broken Mel's heart with an "it's me, not you," then he pushed thoughts of her aside and focused entirely on Emma.

He and Melody had dated all through high school—his parents worried that he'd flush his potential to settle down in rural Indiana, and that would be that. Eli McTilde—Craig's classmate who was always whining about an error in his GPA calculations—would blossom and outshine their one and only son. Eli was, after all, better on the field and court, if not in the classroom. Scholarships were sure to rain down from heaven on that kid. Or, heaven forbid, the elusive Emma Cade—the real brains of their Ben Davis class—would take the cornfields by storm and Craig wouldn't even have a shot at scholarships or cream-of-the-crop residencies.

His parents needn't have worried themselves about any of that, but he couldn't convince them that he indeed had his sights set on Johns Hopkins and the bustle of New York City—not Indianapolis. He and Mel had gone around about their future countless times: where they'd live, their careers, family plans. A real city. Like LA or Chicago. Or New York City. Craig kept pushing, exhausted from the constant push of others in his plans.

Melody was quite content to remain in Hoosier Land, and she had to have known she and Craig were heading in opposite directions. She had to, right? At least that's what he'd told himself in the beginning to ease the guilt.

Though Emma had been in the same classes as Craig year after year, when she showed how much of an adrenaline junkie she was during orientation at Johns Hopkins, it was as if his heart woke up and did a full 180. Melody faded away, and Craig returned the engagement ring he'd meant to give her.

Now, hearing Mel speak Emma's name made him go cold.

"What about Emma? What others?"

Toby, no longer able to "settle," came to the entryway, wagging his black tail so fast and hard that it knocked over a display of doggy deodorant sprays. The bottles went skidding across the floor.

"Toby! No!" The dog had moved from the mess at Craig's feet to greet Melody, nearly knocking over her slender frame as his body brushed against her legs in dopey Labrador affection.

"It's okay." She knelt to pet him, and Toby dropped like a lug and rolled over, exposing his belly.

Craig's head began to throb, and the door chimed again. Diane the Diva was dragging in Winston, an English Bulldog that had clearly enjoyed a mud puddle adventure. Some glob of unknown pink goo stuck to one of his floppy ears, to boot. "You've no idea what kind of morning I've had already, Craig, darling. Please, please. Can you do him up for me pretty today?"

Diane expected top service with no warning or appointment. She'd be better placed smack in a Manhattan high-rise than in an Indy suburb.

Craig stuffed the folder under one arm. Melody looked at him and the chaos in the shop with wide hazel eyes, still rubbing Toby's belly. "Sure. It'll be several hours, given his state." Craig took Winston's leash and Diane air-kissed each of Craig's cheeks with a "thank you, darling" and "Ooh, and another bottle of Uptown Hound, please" and left after she gave a disgusted glance at the mess of bottles on the floor.

Craig inhaled. Exhaled. Squared his shoulders toward Melody. His ER experience should've kicked in, but instead of an adrenaline rush, his heart beat out of rhythm and his mind spun. *Think. Think.* Triage is the rule of law in chaos, separating the life-or-death-right-now situations from the ones that can take a number.

Immediate cases were life and death, requiring action within minutes or seconds. Patients with urgent cases could wait an hour or two, but not much past that. Delayed meant someone needed attention badly, but they'd have to wait their turn—hours or more in most cases, especially if one of the Urgents slid into the critically immediate category.

Golden retriever in the bath, likely getting cold. Poor Max. *Immediate.*

Wrinkled old Bulldog needs isolation and a bath. *Urgent.*

Toby needs to settle. *Delayed.*

Bottles cleaned up. *Really delayed.*

Melody showing up out of the blue? There's no category for that unless confusion counts. And it doesn't.

"I didn't mean to disrupt your whole day, but... I think it's important." She rose, and Toby, unfortunately, greeted Winston with the same exuberance, earning a smear of chunky mud along his flank.

"Toby. Settle!" Craig snapped at the dog. The lab hung his head and went to his bed, muddy flank and all. Another issue in the Delayed column.

"I need your help, Craig. I didn't know where else to go."

He softened and relaxed his shoulders. "Of course. Call you later?"

"My number's in there. There in the front."

"Okay." He watched as she left the shop and turned down the sidewalk. To Winston he said, "C'mon. Let's kennel you up." Winston left a trail of muddy paw prints behind his fat wiggle-walk as they went to the back.

Craig tossed the folder onto a table in the corner. Max barked, still dripping wet and now needing a redo shampoo. Winston barked. Toby whined, not daring to leave his bed. Hackett made his presence known through the too-thin wall separating Wagz from the realty office, his deep woofing no doubt driving Brian nuts.

But the folder's contents were louder in Craig's mind than the ruckus around him. All-consuming. How was he ever to get through the workday?

Craig started back in on Max's coat, trying to focus on the dog and mentally preparing for what he'd need to deal with Winston. Then Toby.

Then Melody Atkins and her manila folder.

3

Melody sat in a back corner booth at The Sicilian in Bella Square and toyed with the red and white checkered tablecloth while she waited for Craig. After a quick phone exchange, Craig said after he closed up Wagz and escorted Toby home, he'd meet her in person.

She beat herself up, replaying their first interaction in over a decade. The pep talks she'd given herself in the Uber and right up to the door of Wagz had failed. As soon as she entered, the emotional flood started. Melody's heart had thumped in her chest from the moment Wagz's doorbell chimed above her head.

And the first thing out of her mouth? What was it? *How've you been?*

And all that babbling? She suppressed an audible moan lest she draw the attention of other diners.

Emma's death had crushed him. A world-class doc turned dog groomer. How'd she think he was doing?

Good grief, Mel.

Melody realized that Emma was the perfect match for

Craig. She'd followed the blurbs and articles the local paper put out about Ben Davis's star academic making it big along with his new wife in NYC. Local Eli McTilde had also gone to the Big Apple, landing a few mentions as a promising new doc Ben Davis would be proud to have back for student convocations and pep talks, but the limelight remained on Dr. & Dr. Thompson. Embracing her heartbreak and runner-up status, Mel flung herself into her courses and only dated occasionally—the most embarrassing a string of bad dinners with Eli. She decided love carried too much risk of bad sushi and even worse company.

When the announcement came that Emma and Craig would grace Blane Park Medical, she took two weeks of accrued time off to avoid processing their hire-on packets. The idea of her snapping their ID badge photos seemed... Well. She took off and never saw either of them around the halls of Human Resources. Not that she didn't sneak a peek into their files to see how those photos turned out when she returned to Blane.

Coward.

Through her nervous fidgeting, the tablecloth started to wrinkle across the table, pulling the condiment caddy to the center and bringing the tabletop décor with it. She smoothed out the cloth, replaced the caddy, and sat on her hands. She needed to get a grip. Craig was off limits, and Melody had no interest in starting anything. Nothing. She'd simply underestimated the effect seeing him for the first time would have on her already fragile mental capacity.

Or perhaps she was misreading everything and fear was having its way with her.

Straight-up terror, actually.

She inhaled and exhaled deeply, concentrating on the

box breathing Dr. Tanberg had worked her through on more than one occasion. She took in her surroundings and tried to relax. The pizzeria was dimly lit, smelled as any other pizzeria smelled, and the speakers serenaded the patrons with cheesy Italian. Only a couple of other tables had diners, for which she was glad.

A waitress came by—Sadie, if her crooked nametag wasn't borrowed—and Mel dismissed her with an "I'm waiting on someone." The gal smiled and checked on the other patrons.

The Sicilian didn't exist when she and Craig were together—most eateries in the newly developed Bella Square fit this bill. She'd chosen it for Craig's benefit, too, not wanting to resurrect memories for him if they dined somewhere that he and Emma had once enjoyed.

You're overthinking, Mel. Get a grip.

The only thing that mattered was the documents she'd snuck out of the hospital's files. Ever since she discovered the connections, Mel regretted signing on with Blane.

All of Indianapolis reeled from the shooting at the Blane Dialysis Center. Again with the trauma center incident.

Then the Marion County Medical Association Award Banquet disaster put the entire city on edge—was nowhere safe?

That one's partly on you, Mel. You chose the venue, after all.

Despite Dr. Tanberg's encouragement since that awful night at the banquet, she couldn't shake the grief she'd single-handedly dealt to The Circle City, leading her to seek legal advice only to be told over and over again that she lacked substantial proof to do anything about it.

No matter that she had no insight into the family chaos happening with the venue's owners.

No matter that the cluster of shootings had been fueled by totally unrelated motives.

No matter that she'd been instructed by her employer to choose one of ten possible locales.

No matter. Her guilt fueled her attempts at reconciling the matter to bring some justice to the whole mess.

Melody aimlessly scrolled her phone, glancing from the screen to the door where Craig would be walking through any moment. She begged her nerves to calm and her hands to stop shaking. When this was over, she'd go home, have a glass of wine, choose a novel from her unapologetically opulent bookshelves (which did not match her Ikea-level decorating skills, but who cares), and settle in with a fluffy blanket and an even fluffier feline.

The evening routine kept her calm and settled, even if barely this side of becoming an alcoholic.

Sadie returned, reaching for the little votive candle next to the caddy and pulled a lighter from her apron pocket. "Are we still waiting, sweetheart?"

Mel wanted to slap the look of pity off the woman's face. She squared her shoulders and sat up straight. "Yes. Still waiting. Just the waters for now, please. And *that* won't be necessary." Mel turned the candle upside down before Sadie could light the wick.

Flickering flames screamed date night. And that's *not* what this was.

Craig appeared from behind the waitress, and Mel's heart sank. He must've come through the back entrance. How much did he see of her fidgeting and near-rudeness with the staff?

Sadie gave Mel a sideways look and left them with two

glasses and menus. Craig slid into the booth across from her. As he settled, she picked up a sweet trace of his cologne—nice, with no hint of wet dog. His face was pale, though, and concern furrowed his brow. He laid the folder next to the upside-down candle.

"Hi."

"Hi." Melody put her phone away and tried to mask her nerves with a gulp of water.

"I'm sorry about this morning. Things got crazy and I—"

"No need for apologies. I should've called first. Given you a heads up."

Impatient, Sadie broke through the pair's awkward pause, asking what they'd like to eat. Craig glanced quickly through the options. Melody ordered a salad, and he chose stromboli.

Not wasting any time with small talk, for which Melody was grateful, Craig tapped the folder. "Where did you get these documents? I understand HIPAA privacy laws and patient confidentiality, but I'm no expert on the human resource side of things. You aren't supposed to have these outside work, right?"

"Blane Park was sued after the first shooting. I accessed invoices and contracts at their request for the legal case. I also signed all kinds of nondisclosure agreements. No big deal. All of this is very regular, and the whole time I thought I was protecting Blane. It was, after all, not Blane's security protocols that had failed, but the new weapons detection security software we purchased from our vendor, Proctor Alliance."

She watched as Craig dug in the folder and came up with a contract agreement between Proctor Alliance and Blane Park. The one that indicated an exclusivity purchasing arrangement that gave steep discounts to the up-and-coming medical facility. Deep, deep discounts.

Mel winced. "To answer your question directly. No. I've no right to possess this information outside of the court order to hand it over after the Blane Dialysis Center shooting. But stuff crosses my desk, and," she lowered her voice to a whisper, "I *noticed* things."

Craig moved the folder to the seat next to him and leaned his head out of the booth before looking both directions. Melody recognized the paranoid gesture. She'd picked up a few of those herself over the last months.

Mel went on, her voice shaking. "Blane Park is huge. You know that. They employ thousands of people and continue to build campuses across the state. They recently signed to expand to three more states over the next five years. They gobble up real estate whether it fits their medical models or not. Some of it feels... off."

"But..." Craig prompted her to go on after she got choked up. Another swallow of water. Another glance into his brown eyes. His hands fiddled with his sweating water glass. For a split second she thought he might reach for her arm. But he didn't.

"Go on..."

"Craig," her voice choked, "Blane Park *knows* Proctor Alliance cuts corners everywhere and they aren't doing anything about it." He sat back, taking his hands out of view, and she sensed the void immediately. She busied herself with her napkin as the waitress brought their food. The stromboli overpowered his cologne and steam rose from the plate.

She picked at her salad with her fork, choosing a bite of tomato and a crouton, then pushed the plate aside. Craig didn't touch his food, either. He brought the folder back to the table and thumbed through the documents.

"You could get in real trouble for having this. Do you have copies?"

"On my phone."

His eyes widened. "Melody—"

"I don't think it's to the point where they're bugging my phone or that I'm being followed. But..."

"But what?"

"When I tried to bring the very first of my concerns to Underwood, he shut me down. He didn't say anything one way or another, but he had that look, right? That look that washes over someone's face when they're being... controlled? Or when—"

His eyes softened. "When they're scared?"

She nodded and continued, spilling out the last few months of discoveries and how she felt like someone was always watching. "Then, last month, they installed ceiling cameras in the HR department—all the individual offices, not just the halls. You know, those little black half-spheres? For security reasons, they said. Proctor Alliance's brand, of course—I have the invoice in the folder. And they upgraded that buggy software so they could detect threats should a disciplined employee become belligerent. Or, or... to call for help if someone in the HR department should have a medical emergency. Like a slip and fall."

"'Slip and fall?' Did it feel like a threat?"

"I don't know. I'm so consumed by this my judgment is off."

Craig finally took a bite of his stromboli, still warm enough that the cheese strung from the fork. Melody made another attempt at her salad. They sat in silence for a long while. Craig occasionally flipped through the folder. She got the feeling he'd memorized every page already—or if not, it soon would be.

"Emma, um." He cleared his throat. "Emma had complained that the quality of the sutures was sub-par. Several snapped during one of her procedures. Sterile gauze pads would arrive half out of their packaging. Stuff that never happened at Mount Lombard. But that's not Proctor Alliance, right? That's another company?"

"No. That's Proctor, too. Everything we get comes through them or one of Proctor's subsidiaries. Sutures. Gauze. Security devices..." Mel explained that Proctor was gaining ground as the go-to supplier for medical complexes in LA, New York, and Chicago. Not to be left out of a great opportunity to rub shoulders with greatness, Underwood wasn't about to see Blane Park of Indianapolis left out of the running. "He's said in more than one board meeting that he hopes the Blane name would one day be synonymous with the likes of The Cleveland Clinic and Mayo."

"And Proctor and the deep discounts would be one way to shortcut to the top."

"Exactly. Craig, Emma deserves justice. They all do. But I don't have it in me to be a whistleblower. I've been told by multiple attorneys that I don't have enough to connect the dots to the actual shootings since those were separate incidents and all separate, personal motives on the part of the shooters. Not a too-new-too-soon software issue." She covered her face with both hands and slunk into the booth. "I'm so selfish. I just want a quiet life."

"That's what you've always wanted, and you deserve to have that."

"I thought maybe..." she nodded at Craig.

Craig's eyebrows shot up. "Maybe *I* could blow the whistle?" Craig stiffened and in that instant, Mel regretted ever walking into Wagz. What was she thinking? Of course he didn't want to get involved.

He'd moved on.

Gained some closure, even if that meant working as a dog groomer, which is more than she could say of the closure she'd grasped at after Craig had devastated her imagined future.

The flicker of hope Melody dared to have seconds before she handed Craig this mess sputtered out like a candle flame with no access to oxygen. She had about as much faith in this crusade of hers as the upside-down votive on the table spontaneously combusting.

"Craig, I'm sorry. I shouldn't have—" She wiped fiercely at an unwelcome flood of tears and stiffened.

His shoulders sunk. "I've moved— I mean, I've not moved on. But Emma's family. And dragging them through this. All these families. I know... I *know* they want to move on." He closed the folder, shoving wayward pages back into the manila cover. "This certainly needs looking into, but I'm not—"

"You don't have to—"

Craig looked Mel dead in the face. His brown eyes held so much pain and confusion. What had she done?

"I don't think I can even if I wanted to," he finally said after taking a deep breath. Craig threw some cash from his wallet onto the table—enough to cover the dinner twice over —and stood to leave. "Sorry, Mel."

"It's okay."

He nodded awkwardly and turned and left.

Mel sat frozen for a few minutes, mentally beating herself up over bringing this to him. She looked at the remnants of their disastrous dinner, complete with the upside-down candle, but then took in a quick breath of hope. She ducked her head under the table to scan the opposite seat.

No folder.

She exhaled and rose back up, her ribs shaking as the air left her lungs.

He took the folder.

4

CRAIG WALKED HOME, his head spinning. In any other circumstance, no matter how the evening would've gone, he'd have escorted his dinner mate to their car or waited with them for their ride to show.

But he couldn't.

He couldn't breathe, and he couldn't watch her tears fall.

His walk was ten blocks, and he was glad the night was crisp enough to dry the sweat and clear his lungs. He may have held his breath for most of the dinner. The heavy Italian dish was a poor choice given how stressed he was, and he'd only taken a few bites.

It was unfair. All of it. That Emma died in the first place. That any of the victims had. That Blane Park—a place the pair of them had been so proud to call their employer—was so greedy that it was risking the lives of its employees and patients to cut a few bucks off its bills.

That Melody had been dragged into this.

That Blane Park CEO Alfred Underwood, who'd welcomed Emma and him with open arms and fanfare, was

25

the kind of man who refused to look objectively at a very real problem.

Poor Mel.

That she had blindsided Craig with something so emotionally charged miffed him—and not just a little bit. But she was distraught and had carried the burden for too long. This was all very Erin Brockovich, and Melody, though capable and intelligent, was no Erin.

He wasn't sure he was an Erin, either.

Emma would've been...

He paused at a crosswalk and checked that the folder was still tucked tightly under his arm. An uneasy sensation crept down the back of his neck, and he couldn't help but turn around, scanning the street and sidewalk for prying eyes. He'd done the same thing more than once at The Sicilian.

Nope. Not an Erin.

As soon as Craig entered the foyer of his small bungalow, Toby greeted him as only a Labrador could, barely allowing Craig to toss his keys and Wagz's keycard into the authentic Aztec pottery piece that he and Emma had scored on their trip to South America. He'd thought the bowl hideous. "It doesn't match anything we own."

"Nothing we own matches." Then Emma blinked at him and grinned, and that was all it took for the piece to have a prominent home in their foyer.

God, help him. Everything reminded him of her. Snippets of conversation would return to him in dibs and drabs. Or gushing fountains.

Toby at his heels, Craig tossed the folder on the kitchen counter, then thought better of it and took it to the bedroom, where he stuffed it deep under the mattress of his always-unmade bed.

Kneeling on the floor, that same sense of dread from the street struck Craig again, this time in the pit of his stomach.

Melody said she had copies on her phone.

He fished his phone from his pocket, and his thumb hovered over her contact. He should call her and tell her to delete them. Or tell her to get a new phone entirely.

But Craig had called Mel earlier to set a time for dinner. Maybe *he* should get a new phone for even having called her.

No, no. What if she deletes her digital files and then his house burns down along with the hard copies?

Good grief, breathe. You aren't even going to act on this. You're moving on, remember?

Moving on. Ha.

More like two steps forward, ten steps back. And the folder's contents threatened to send him to the pit of despair that he'd been trying desperately to dig out of for years.

What was it Brian had said to him the first day he'd brought Hackett to Rivers Realty?

Something about the flavor of grief?

Craig slumped to the floor, pulled his knees to his chest, and put his head in his hands, recalling that conversation in vivid detail—a skill he had sharpened in the trauma bays. The ability to replay events for charting and relaying information to colleagues was invaluable. Back then, though, he never had to slump on the floor.

Now he used recall as a coping mechanism.

Toby settled next to him with a whimper.

"Some life events resurrect the grief. The flavor changes and it's served up with a different side dish every time."

Brian's brother, a decorated police officer, died in the line of duty before Emma and Craig moved to Indianapolis. Brian inherited the funeral plans—and Hackett. The

Realtor also earned a full head of white hair at the ripe age of twenty-nine as a thank you very much from the universe. He'd left his hometown of Straughn to distance himself from the hard memories and started Rivers Realty.

"I don't know how you do it." Craig didn't know how anyone could put one foot in front of the other after such a devastating loss. Craig felt like he was on autopilot, relying on Emma's ghost to dictate his daily agenda. He didn't know if Brian's brother had a ghost.

"How does anyone do it?" Brian shrugged and offered to scratch Hackett's head. The shepherd ducked Brian's fingers and walked away indifferently. Brian laughed. "Treats and tennis balls. And a lot of counseling. For me. Not him." Brian crooked his head toward Hackett, his face clouded. "When Hackett crosses the veil to be with Randy, well." He shrugged.

Mel and the Blane Park fiasco was certainly a different flavor with a whole lot of complicated side dishes. But counseling wasn't something Craig had ever entertained. He knew enough of brain anatomy and psychology to understand PTSD. He also knew that, with time, his grief would subside.

Should subside, had Craig not given it a home where it could grow roots and scale his ribs like stubborn ivy up the side of a brick building.

He rose from the bedroom floor, sweat starting at the back of his neck, his hands shaking. He stared down at the bed. How could his nerves of steel become frayed so badly in such a short time? It wasn't that long ago that he oversaw entire trauma teams with ticking clocks and lives in the balance as the break-neck pace of the Big Apple rushed around him.

Move him to the cornfield, and within a few short years, he's a puddle of anxiety.

How pathetic.

He began fidgeting with the covers, and Toby thought they were playing their typical flip-the-sheet and peek-a-boo, and started bounding on and off the mattress. But Craig wanted something to control, even if that meant making the bed. He shooed the dog away, straightened the sheets, and righted the pillows parallel to the bookcase headboard. The cubby above Emma's side of the bed still held her novel-in-progress, a legal crime thriller bookmarked with a takeout menu from La Parada. He'd not opened it or bothered to put it back on the bookshelf in the living room. Occasionally, he'd take a dry cloth and wipe the dust from the cover, but otherwise he left the book undisturbed.

"What would she do, Tobes? What would Emma do, huh?" Craig rolled a rogue tennis ball that had dislodged from the bed-making into the living room.

Whenever Craig caught one of his fresh-from-the-classroom med students in the ER frozen, either at their first glimpse of real gore or from the sheer chaos that a full house of critical patients always brings, Craig would grab them by the arm and say, "Remember your training. Breathe. Block out everything else. Then move."

That's what he needed to do now. Breathe. Block. Move.

Breathe. Focus on calming techniques he'd used on families in the waiting rooms across the nation and with his patients. He called Toby to him and rubbed his hands over the lab's coat. He could feel his pulse slow and his mind calm. Screw counseling. He had no time.

Block. Block out the folder. Block out the look on Mel's face when she realized he'd been the wrong choice to bring this to. He didn't have the willpower and it wouldn't change the outcome. Emma would still be dead. So would the others.

Move.

Toby dropped the slobbered-on ball into Craig's lap. He jostled the dog's ears and rolled the ball again.

Craig was moving on.

MEL GULPED down the last lukewarm sips of her coffee and slumped into her office chair. After leaving The Sicilian last night, she'd Ubered home and sobbed, sending Omega scampering for a saner corner of the house.

She'd poured herself a glass of wine, was too brain fuddled to read, and allowed herself one last mental thrashing over the entire day with Craig. Enough crying. Enough digging.

She'd sought outside counsel and reached out to Craig. No one could say she didn't try, and what more was there to do? What would Dr. Tanberg Say? *You have to stop this spinning, Mel. There's nothing more you can do.*

She'd gone to bed exhausted and awoke in the same state, wondering if it would've made a difference had she spilled to Craig about therapy and Eli and... No matter. None of it mattered. *Stop spinning.*

After throwing on the simplest of professional outfits, she ordered her ride and arrived at Blane Park Human Resources Department ready to face yet another Tuesday.

She glanced over her shoulder at the half-moon camera —that was only there in case someone should need assistance.

Yup. Just another Tuesday.

She logged into her computer and entered the long-string password for her email. Routine stuff, mostly. New hires. Job posting updates. Contracts for physicians.

But one stuck out, stamped urgent.

She clicked on the subject line. *Need your help—fundraising.* Riki in the marketing department shouldn't need Mel's help with fundraising.

The email opened, and she stood, knocking her thermos onto the floor as her heart slammed into her ribcage.

Hey, Mel.
Mr. Underwood said you were my go-to for suppliers for our next big event. Mr. Underwood wants to, and I quote the Big Guy here, "increase Blane's brand throughout the expanding communities of our Indianapolis neighborhoods." He wants us to see about hosting in Bella Square or Candle View, one of the other newer areas, if we can. He said you've orchestrated stuff like this before. Pitched the idea of a Caring Hands Banquet to him and he liked it. But, we need to move fast on this. Mr. Underwood says some "pretty impressive donors" will be in town, and we want to get the ball rolling.

She barely read the rest of the message and, instead, picked up the phone to call Riki.

"Hey, woman!" Riki's standard greeting when she knew the caller.

"Hey, Riki." Mel's response wasn't so cheery. "What's this about another event?"

"Another? OMG! Have we already done one of these things?"

Mel took a deep breath. "Depends on what you mean by 'one of these things.' The last banquet Blane Park was a part of didn't, well..." Mel trailed off, hoping Riki would catch a clue.

"Oh. Oh. You mean the Vanderbilt shooting. Oh, good grief, no. That wouldn't happen again. And besides, that night had nothing to do with Blane. I mean, not really. Mr. Underwood was scheduled to receive an award, but the shooting... That was random. Right? One guy ticked at the owner of the venue? Family stuff? Yeah? Blane was not to blame. No way. That's a rogue instance." Riki's rambling showed how new she was to the area and how little insight she carried into the gravity of that fateful night.

Mel said nothing. She struggled to hold the receiver to her ear, her palm sweaty and hand shaky. Riki didn't know Mel was the one who'd set the whole thing up. Chosen Vanderbilt as the venue.

But Underwood did.

Was this a test? To keep quiet? To see if Mel would do as she was told? She felt the half-moon circle in the corner of her office glare at her. Studying. Waiting.

"So, anyway. Underwood said you were the go-to for all things venue set-up. Said you were a guru with this sort of stuff."

Underwood said, Underwood said. "I have a master's degree in human resources. Not one lick of training in event planning." She snapped her reply. Mel *could* help, but she certainly wasn't about to. She wanted nothing to do with this or any other fanfare outside Blane's main campus—or within it. She took a deep breath and gathered herself.

Be diplomatic. Be blameless. This might be a test...

"What Underwood means, I think, is that I would have been your contact for vendors—you know, the humans— that you'll need to staff and cater and such, but now—"

Riki didn't let her finish. "Gotcha. If you could send me the list of approved ones. And where do I get the... Oh. Oh. I found what I was looking for. Duh. Never mind. I see here we have a contract. Anything we can get from Proctor, they give us a discount and... I suppose they're our Man Behind the Curtain, making all the magic happen. Hey! That helps our margin for the fundraiser portion—" Riki droned on and Mel zoned out. She hadn't looked at the contracts since pulling documents for legal, afraid to log in to that section of the system to see if anything had changed.

Riki confirmed it.

Nothing had changed. Proctor was Blane's go-to "guy."

A freaking wizard, even, for another event supplied with Proctor equipment—be it folding chairs or chafing dishes to keep the "impressive donor's" crab cakes warm. Or state-of-the-art weapons detection.

Hosted by Blane.

"Sorry again to bother. I'll see you around? Maybe at the banquet?"

Mel shook off her haze. "Maybe. No worries."

She hung up the receiver and turned to her monitor. She hovered the mouse over the trash icon in the email.

You have to stop this spinning, Mel. There's nothing more you can do.

But there was something.

She moved the mouse a fraction of an inch to the left and clicked print.

6

CROWN HILL CEMETERY was Emma Thompson's final resting place and Toby's favorite place in the world, especially when the air is chilly and enough fallen leaves for the dog to roll and romp in. As soon as there was a break at Wagz Tuesday afternoon, Craig loaded up Toby and off they went.

Craig drove his Jeep through the entire property, starting on the north side of 38th Street, scanning for active funerals or large groups. He didn't want to be disrespectful, especially if Toby were to take a spell barking at a squirrel.

The massive cemetery used to sit on the outskirts of Indy, but over the years, the city grew up on all sides, fencing in the five-hundred-plus acres and thousands upon thousands of graves.

Craig was in so much shock after the shooting that he acquiesced when Emma's parents offered her a spot in the family plot. She was laid to rest in one of the four they'd secured years before. Two were already spoken for, but as yet unoccupied by Mr. and Mrs. Cade, and Alex Cade,

Emma's brother, had been resting in the third for quite some time.

All the death that Emma and Craig witnessed in their line of work should've prompted them to secure final arrangements, but they didn't. Youth and adrenaline probably had a lot to do with it.

Flying from New York to Indiana to put Alex in the ground after his passing didn't provoke them to action either.

It didn't dawn on Craig that he and Emma wouldn't be eternally together until months after the funeral. The chances of him securing a plot within shouting distance of the Cade family were slim to none.

Another pass around Emma's section, and Craig saw no mourners or active services, so he let Toby loose from the confines of the Jeep. The dog spun with glee as Craig neared Emma's grave, like Toby simply knew. Toby also somehow knew not to do his business near the headstones. Craig trusted Toby would, as always, hold it until they reached a nearby cluster of trees before marking anything. Craig always had a supply of pooper-scooper bags in his pocket, but Toby preferred the comforts of his own backyard for that business.

After visiting Alex, Emma and Craig often walked the cemetery, visiting James Whitcomb Riley's spot. Many other walks in the "urban green space" revealed the final resting spots of the admired like President Benjamin Harrison to those the likes of John Dillinger. They'd walk and walk, admiring Indy's skyscrapers in the distance as the sun set. Crown Hill was a far cry from Central Park for a thousand reasons, but they'd found the solitude here a welcome relief from particularly rough days at Blane Park.

"Maybe we should be in the Community Mausoleum."

Craig had suggested. He'd found the marble-lined interior and the stained-glass installations rather impressive.

"Too tight of a space for me. No thanks." And that's the extent of what Craig had known of Emma's wishes.

After a visit to the trees and his usual lap around the section, Toby returned to the Jeep. Craig retrieved the single white long-stemmed rose from the dashboard, and they walked a few rows over to Emma's grave.

Even before he reached the edge of her family's section, Craig could see someone had already placed fresh flowers on Emma's headstone. Toby hastened his step, nose to the ground, zigging and zagging on someone's recent trail.

"Who was it? Granny? Gramps?" Emma's parents frequently visited their deceased children. Once in a while, Craig would come with them, but less and less as of late, despite the pangs of guilt over pulling away. He preferred these moments to himself and chalked it up to moving on.

And having space to breathe.

Toby circled Emma's headstone. A bundle of grocery-store flowers in purples and lavenders leaned against her name—this would be the third or fourth time Craig had found such bouquets here in the last few weeks. On another circle around, Toby's tail knocked them over, and Craig bent to right the bouquet, smelling their sweetness before replacing them. It wasn't like Emma's parents to leave such generic blooms. They usually brought roses or, sometimes in the spring, tulips.

Alex's grave got sunflower stems.

A thought crashed into his mind. *Mel wouldn't be the one...*

Before Craig could process the idea, Toby's head whipped up, as if catching a scent on the wind itself and gave a bark. Before Craig could utter the "heel" command,

Toby was off, ripping through the rows, headed for a couple of figures in the distance, tail wagging.

"Toby, stop! Come!"

Craig's heart sped up, and he took off after him, grateful Toby'd put on the brakes and returned to his master before ramming snout-first into the people ahead.

The pair turned, and Craig, slightly out of breath from the sprint, held what little air he had left, still clutching his long-stemmed rose.

Joel Hartley. A foot taller, lean and spry and filled with life. The lady with him must be his mother. Her eyes brightened when she recognized Craig.

"Doctor Thompson."

Craig exhaled and tried to return her smile. He focused on Toby for a few seconds to gather himself.

"Ma'am."

He turned to the child—now more the shape of a young man than the broken little car accident boy Emma had saved.

"Doctor Thompson." The kid's voice cracked. Craig didn't know if it was from emotion or pre-puberty voice squeaks. Toby ran to Joel, whacking his tail against the boy's legs.

"I hope we aren't bothering you." The mother—Mrs. Hartley—watched as her son bent to love on Toby. The lab slathered kisses all over the boy's face, making him laugh and fall to his butt on the cold ground.

"No. No. I..." Craig gathered himself further. "Thank you. For the flowers, I mean. She'd love them."

"We'd moved away for a time. Too many awful memories. But my parents are aging, and, well. Back home again in Indiana."

"I know the feeling—and the song." Craig shifted

awkwardly. The mother and son were dressed simply. That they spent their likely meager funds on memorial flowers for Emma touched him. He felt guilty about classifying the flowers as generic. "They are nice. Very pretty."

"Joel always picks out purple ones. Miss Emma—that's what he calls her, Miss Emma, had on purple scrubs that day—" Mrs. Hartley's eyes fell to the rose in his hand.

Craig nodded in understanding, not wanting to know if the mom would finish that sentence with "the day she died" or "the day she saved Joel."

Joel rose, having his fill of the dog and returned to his mom's side. "She's my hero. I think about her every day, Doctor. Every day."

Craig smiled and reached to shake his hand. "Me too, me too."

"Well, we'll leave you to it then." Mom put her arm around Joel, and they made their way through the grave rows away from Craig.

Toby and Craig returned to Emma. Craig was going to lay the rose on top of the headstone, then thought better of it. He wasn't going to show up Joel's purple bouquet, even with a single stem. He stepped a few feet to the left and placed the white rose on Alex's grave instead. Alex would've rolled his eyes, but Emma would approve, he thought.

At least of the rose, not of Craig's cowardice.

She's my hero.

Craig was no hero.

He dropped to his knees. Toby sat next to him, leaning into Craig's shoulder. Craig traced the letters of Emma's name etched in the cold granite.

Emma wouldn't have abandoned Mel in the restaurant.

She wouldn't have smushed a folder full of evidence under the mattress.

She would've stood up. In her purple scrubs, and despite all odds, she'd have fought for the victims.

She wouldn't have needed time to breathe or block.

She'd be a force.

From the second the problem presented itself, his Emma would've *moved*.

Craig's Jeep took care of the short drive back to Wagz as if it had state-of-the-art autopilot. Toby was zonked out after their mid-morning cemetery break and lay curled up in the passenger seat. Craig was in a funk.

He pulled into the spot behind the strip mall and sat for a bit, head leaning against the rest. Craig had spent many moments in this lot, gazing out over the ever-expanding Bella Square neighborhood. Emma would've liked the way it had progressed, he thought. The dog grooming business. Being closer to her parents. Interacting with people and pets. A pace that would've allowed for the couple to raise a child.

Craig would've liked it right along with her. But on his own? He wasn't so sure. He never imagined himself in a future without Emma in it.

He only knew how to navigate life now with Emma's ghost.

Wagz had four appointments this afternoon, and, given the emotional interaction at the cemetery, Craig was hardly in the mood for the dirty dogs—and definitely not in the mood for their humans. Toby stirred and nudged Craig's arm with his muzzle.

"Time to go back to work, huh, Tobes?"

The dog thumped his tail against the seat. Craig reached over and popped the door open for him. Toby bounded out, relieved himself in the stretch of grass lining the back lot, and headed for the back door as Craig stretched and fished the door key out of his pocket.

When Craig looked up from the keyring, he saw something flapping from the back door, about eye level. Probably a new startup plastering fliers for a grand opening. That happened a lot in this developing area where small business owners relied on one another to spread the word.

Craig took a few more steps. That was no marketing material.

Duct-taped to the back door was an envelope with CRAIG scrawled in black ink across the middle and Blane Park's logo in the return address section.

The duct tape had pulled a quarter-sized patch of paint off Wagz's back door. As irrelevant as that detail was, it irritated him. Easier to focus on something mundane than yet another piece of the Blane Park tragedy.

The envelope held a handwritten letter from Mel and a printout of an email.

Craig. I heard what you said last night, and I get your position. But this came across my desk this morning and thought you should be aware. I can't help but wonder if they copied me on the email when they

didn't need to, given as much grief as I've handed them about the weapons detection software, that this must be some sort of test. From Underwood? From Legal? I can't be sure.
Maybe you could file it with the rest of the documents in your folder…

Mel

She was relentless. *File it with the rest…*
Your folder.

Mel had no idea the turmoil he was putting himself through over this, but she had to know exactly what *that* jab would do to him.

Good grief. He *had* brought the folder home after he said he wanted nothing to do with any rogue investigation. He hadn't even thought about it. Just scooped it from the booth and out the door it went with him.

So there's that.

That was on him.

So was the fact that he'd made Toby wait in the Jeep while he ran back into Wagz after their day's appointments were done to retrieve a box of thumbtacks from his office desk drawer.

So was the fact that he placed a Door Dash order from La Parada, a quesadilla and salsa. "Brain food. For hard questions." Emma had said that about the Mexican spots they'd enjoyed in New York. Whenever they had a dilemma with a patient one of them had chosen to keep tabs on past the ER. Or whenever they were dreaming. Or when her brother died and they needed to decide how to help out her parents.

He and Toby had only been back to their bungalow for a half hour before the bell rang with the takeout. Craig took the sack and thanked the delivery kid. Toby bumped his leg all the way back to the kitchen until Craig plated the food and tossed the dog a tortilla chip.

"Time to get to work." Toby looked at him with a tilted head. The dog equated "work" with "Wagz," so Craig clarified as he took a bite of the steak quesadilla and washed it down with sweet tea. "Brain work." He finished the whole meal standing up in the kitchen, then turned to the bedroom.

Determined to find focus and a direction, Craig breathed. He needed to block out everything else. Emma's essence all through the condo. Melody and the history they shared. The scene from the cemetery that day with its purple grocery store bouquet.

He retrieved the folder from between the mattress and spread the contents over the kitchen island. He began taking down framed photos from the wall—careful not to dwell on Emma's face in any of them. He leaned them behind the television stand so Toby's tail wouldn't smash into the glass.

Craig then set about tacking up page after page of Blane Park and Proctor Alliance documents. All over the wall.

On top of it all he tacked the note from Mel, right in the middle. For good measure, he stuck the now-empty envelope with the duct tape still attached off to the side. So he'd remember to rib her about the marred paint job.

"Toby!" The dog happily heeled and followed Craig to the couch, where the two of them settled down with Toby draped over Craig's lap. Craig used the dog's side as a desktop, frequently looking up at the wall. He scribbled notes from the conversation with Melody.

He noted bits of conversations he'd had with Emma over their shared concerns about shoddy surgical and wound care supplies. He documented seeing Joel Hartley and his mom at the cemetery—more to keep him grounded in the "why" of the matter than anything else.

The furnace kicked on, sending the edges of the papers blowing softly against the wall and making a faint rustling sound. Toby let out a contented sigh.

Back on the notes, Craig continued to write.

Find a secure location for files—after he committed them to memory. The wall was a temporary workstation, at best. *Immediate.*

Meet with Mel. Discreetly. Discuss phone security concerns and how they could communicate without raising suspicion. *Urgent.*

Craig scratched Toby's head as he thought. The dog's tail thumped gently against the couch in a quiet rhythm. "What are we gonna do about Wagz while Daddy runs amok blowing whistles and dodging shadows?" Toby whined and sighed. Craig agreed.

On his pad, he wrote: Hire a part-time dog groomer. *Delayed. No. Urgent?*

At that last line, a pit formed in Craig's stomach. He didn't want to hand Wagz's keys to anyone. But he couldn't tackle Blane Park and keep Wagz's schedule all while holding onto any semblance of sanity.

Urgent it is.

The handwritten letter from Mel flapped the most when the furnace blew, demanding more attention than anything else. He wrote Melody's name in block letters, tracing it over and over as his mind spun. That spot at the base of his ribs where he held onto all of his grief trembled. It had been a long time. She was a mess. Could he trust her?

Was she telling him everything? He hoped so. He thought so. She seemed genuine in her concern over the matter.

But during their strained dinner, she'd start to say something, take a breath, then back up and start again. More than once. Was she being as transparent as possible? Alex did that. Emma's brother seemed to want to say what was on his mind, then come to find out after his death, he had harbored gobs of secrets that had eventually done him in. So sad.

Was Mel doing the same thing, or had Craig become paranoid? There was no one following him on the street—but deeply kept secrets could cause more damage than a midnight mugging. What to do about Mel?

He closed his eyes, and visions of Emma flooded his mind. Their courtship. Their wedding day. Emma's arms wrapped around Toby as she waited for Craig to join them in bed. Her in her scrubs, pacing with him on the ambulance bay, ready to spring into life-saving action.

The art she hung on the walls of their condo. Her cosmetic drawer in the bathroom full of toiletries. The magnets she collected on every vacation they took still hanging on the fridge.

The Aztec bowl in the foyer.

The unread novel in the headboard.

He drug himself from the haze. Next to Mel's name, in bigger block caps, he wrote, *Delayed.*

Thought better of it. Drew a line through *Delayed* and scribbled *Nope.*

8

"He'll be applying Monday."

"That seems fast." Dr. Tanberg sat across the room from Mel, his usual spot in the black leather recliner. He never popped the legs up during their sessions, but she wondered if he did after she left to write in his notebook or nap between patients. The odd things you think about at the exact second you're pouring your soul out to your therapist...

Sometime during her first month of visits, Mel had felt along the edge of the matching black leather couch she sat on, feeling for the reclining handle. There wasn't one. She supposed patients were expected to lie down if needed, not recline their feet.

"I'm glad to have it started, I think. Terrified at the same time."

"Dr. Thompson didn't want to come back, though, did he? Didn't he refuse your initial request?"

She cringed and told him about the email she'd taped to his door.

"That's a tad passive-aggressive for you, Mel."

"I don't disagree." When someone holds a mirror to your behavior, what are you to do but acknowledge the reflection?

Dr. T. didn't dwell on the issue. "You've waited quite a long time to approach him with your findings. And, for whatever reason, he's in. So, what are you scared of, exactly?"

Mel hesitated. "Everything" is what she wanted to say, but she'd been playing this game too long to try to slip that past Doc.

"Working with him. In the same building as Eli. That nothing will be found. That something will be found." She hesitated. "Everything."

Mel hoped this therapy session with Dr. Tanberg would help address her conflicted emotions and get some tips on how to remain professional and, quite frankly, distant during this transition working with Craig. She was always grateful for Tanberg's advice, and today more than usual, the trusted therapist seemed to hang on her every word at this new turn of events in her life.

Mel supposed she'd been a rather dull patient. Cat. Books. Linda. Wine (hoping Dr. T. wouldn't declare her a functioning alcoholic—he hadn't, yet) because she needed to deal with Linda. Paper shuffling. And seeing that Doc's patients were mostly from the Blane Park Medical Campus —all of whom had similar traumas from the shootings, a little office espionage with an ex-love was... what? Exciting?

"Do you believe you have feelings for Dr. Thompson, Craig, rather?"

"No." Mel answered quickly, the image of the upside-down candle on the checkered tablecloth at The Sicilian came to mind, so she focused on the photos of Dr. T. and his buddies that were tacked along the bookshelves. Lots of nice cars in those pictures. She was still Ubering everywhere—

"And Eli? Any leftovers there?"

Mel jerked back and felt her eyes widen in horror. "Oh, god no."

Dr. T. laughed and jotted a couple of notes on his ledger. "But these two men under the same roof..."

"It's odd. I guess. And it's not even the point. I shouldn't even be focused there. The shootings are the focus. Why they happened. My role—"

In rare form, Dr. T. cut her off. "Mel. You are not to blame for Vanderbilt. You were doing your job and have no control over random acts of cowardice or vengeance performed at the hands of others."

"But I should've seen the connection."

"A connection that hasn't been proven yet. May never be proven and may not have played a role at all." Dr. T. had to see Mel was escalating. Breathing increasing. Fidgeting.

"Let's walk through the box breathing again."

She rolled her eyes at him, but after a few cycles of that, she felt calmer and more grounded.

"I suggest you write down a list of next steps and tackle one at a time, focusing your energy instead of allowing your mind to wander from random issue to random issue. What do you think is the next most important step to take now that you've handed the folder over?"

Mel thought for a moment, a million thoughts swirling until she landed on one. "Process Craig's new hire paperwork."

"Which is a task you've completed hundreds of times for others, yes?"

"Yes."

"And a win with that task would look like..."

"A win would be to process the paperwork without giving the reason for Craig's presence away."

"And this will happen..."

"Monday."

"So between now and Monday, what will you do?"

"Drink wine and stay home with my cat."

Dr. T. laughed, Mel joined in, but she didn't think her response was funny. That straight-up was her intention. "Find something productive to do with your time so your mind doesn't dwell on worries that will never materialize."

At one point months ago, Dr. T. told her evidence of Blane and Proctor's role in the shootings or even a software error wouldn't likely materialize—how could it when neither business was at fault? But now Craig had a rather hefty file in his possession. Mel pushed this aside.

After a few more exchanges on family matters, the standard "How is Omega, anyway?", and the obligatory warning to watch her alcohol consumption, their session ended. Dr. T. handed Mel his business card. Mel was confused.

"What's this?"

"That has my personal number. On the back. Text me anytime in case things take a turn and you need a quick answer to something between sessions. I don't want any of this to derail the hard work you've done in therapy all these years."

Mel stared, dumbfounded at the all-elusive "text me whenever" offer. She'd only ever heard of him doing that with one other person, and that was an actual first-account witness to the Vanderbilt disaster who was dealing with severe PTSD issues.

She thanked him and made her way out of the building, past the other therapists' offices to the main foyer where a dozen patients, from other Blane Park Medical head-cases much like Mel to war vet amputees, waited for the elevators.

By the time her Uber pulled up to the front of the building, Mel already had Dr. Tanberg's direct number keyed into her contacts and flagged as a favorite.

The only favorite in her phone.

9

JORDAN PROCTOR ROLLED into the prosthesis office in his electric scooter after handing over his crutches to the doorman in the downstairs lobby of his penthouse apartment. He and the doorman had an understanding on his prosthesis appointment days—take the crutches, charge the scooter, and ready the accessible van. Jordan left his malfunctioning prosthetic in his penthouse, stacked in the back corner of a closet with three others nearly identical to it. He was going through legs faster now than in the eight years since he'd last seen his left foot.

Unfortunately, a lookup of the serial number on the parts told Jordan exactly why he'd gone through so many, but he pushed the thought aside.

Blane Park's three-story medical outbuilding wasn't at all well thought out. Slapping a Caring Hands logo on the front of the dilapidated structure didn't go with Blane's brand, in Jordan's opinion. And Proctor Alliance, his pride-and-joy company supplying anything and everything a medical complex could ever hope for, was all about partnering with only the best.

No. This look didn't bode well at all.

It was decided in the joint meeting between Blane Park's Alfred Underwood and Proctor Alliance's expansion team, buildings such as this were either:

A. Slotted for demolition for the eyesores they are,

B. Scheduled for major renovations using Proctor Alliance's army of corporations to supply building materials, or

C. Procured for reasons personal to Jordan.

That last point was only for property in Indiana, though. Points A and B held true for other regions in the States.

Jordan prided himself on thinking through every eventuality in his businesses—right down to the tile selection for the bathroom backsplashes, and he expected others to do the same. Who in their right mind would've put a prosthesis office on a third floor in a building with outdated elevators barely big enough for a regular wheelchair and whoever might be pushing it, let alone a more modernized scooter with a turn radius of a semi-truck?

He'd brought this problem up with his board. Never wanting to disappoint Mr. Jordan Proctor the Third, they offered to set up the prosthesis clinic in the brand-spanking new Blane Park Medical main campus building—even before Jordan bought his plane ticket to Indy and ordered Two Men and a Truck for the haul to the Midwest. He'd refused to relocate the clinic, instead envisioning a completely new facility one hundred percent dedicated to prostheses of every kind—arms, legs, eyes... you name it. Physical therapy suites equipped with top-of-the-line equipment and the best and brightest talent from the top schools to help those with a little less body mass to adapt.

As he wrestled the scooter through yet another just-wide-enough door, he's not sure why he didn't acquiesce to the main campus. Since coming west, he'd been forced to take time from his schedule to cater to his stump way more often than anyone with his status should. His four years in Indiana have proven that he belongs elsewhere—Manhattan to be exact. Where folks know how to innovate.

Eyes on the prize, Jordan. Stay focused on the goal.

Jordan signed in with the receptionist, who alerted his prosthetist immediately. "Mr. Proctor is here, Keith." Jordan nodded at her and navigated toward the window for his short wait. Keith knew better than to leave him. The view out the window showcased barren fields, the local farmers had already harvested corn and soybeans, leaving a patchwork of nothingness. Nothingness in the Crossroads of America that Jordan wanted to help Blane Park—and himself—turn into more money than anyone could ever dream...

Jordan rubbed his upper thighs, working out the knots that inevitably happen when his posture is askew. After nearly a decade with only one leg, you'd think visits to have his silicone stump cover replaced and the rotator joint adjusted would be second nature.

But they weren't.

With every prosthetic follow-up, Jordan fought not to relive the trauma all over again—and during every agonizing physical therapy session with his private specialist. Perhaps the layout of this building had something to do with it. One must pass amputees sweating in agony in their open therapy room with glass windows facing the hallway leading up to the consultation areas.

One must also pass the prosthesis lab with the same glass facade where one could observe techs busily assembling and reassembling legs, arms, hips, etc., to be worn by someone who suffered great loss.

"It came in last night on the late delivery, Mr. Proctor." Keith was proud of himself. The kid had worked hard, at least as hard as he could, to diagnose the issue with the faulty left legs and fashion Jordan a totally new device from the toes up. "We used state-of-the-art materials. I apologize that nothing I used in this piece came from Proctor Alliance's database, so we couldn't assemble it here in our labs, but you said—"

Jordan cut him off. "I'm perfectly aware they aren't in our database." Once he had Keith look up the serial numbers of the rotator mechanism, the pylon support, and the silicone stump sleeve, it had become evident to Jordan what the problem was. He insisted the kid source out 'the latest and greatest,' no matter the supplier, and "Proctor will add that line of prosthetic to our supply. We only want the best for our patients, after all." He softened. "Keith, you did a great job, I'm sure."

Keith helped Jordan stand on his right leg, drop his custom-tailored pants to the floor, and hop out of them. Those pants came from the best tailor in New York City, an older guy who'd clothed five-star generals. The tailor made the heroes, well, not look like they encountered hell. The fabric flowed and moved around his fake leg, and most of the time, no one ever gave Jordan's lower limbs anything more than a passing glance—and only then to admire his creases.

"Steady yourself here with the bar. Yep, that's right, you know the drill." Keith dressed a blister on Jordan's stump. "No wearing this at home. Let it get some air, sir."

"Yeah. I know that drill, too."

The tech slid a new, smooth silicone sleeve over Jordan's

stump, and then, with a satisfying slurp, the socket suctioned onto the silicone sleeve, perfectly fitting the stump. "Wow. Wow." Jordan began putting weight on it, slowly letting go of the grab bar. "What a huge difference."

Keith beamed. "You were right to order nothing but the best materials."

Jordan thought of the stack of legs in his closet—all made with Proctor Alliance parts. His race to see Proctor Alliance reach the Fortune 100 would be his own downfall if he wasn't careful. "Yes. Proctor Alliance will definitely have to source those parts." But he knew his company wouldn't. These parts would be too expensive to turn a quick profit on. Jordan himself wouldn't even approve of the acquisition.

This leg would have to last him, lest it become necessary to waste precious mental energy concocting a cover story for Keith when the tech couldn't find these exact parts in the Proctor Alliance catalog.

And no one could ever know about the pile of left leg failures back at the penthouse.

"Keith?" The prosthetist was resetting his workstation for the next patient as Jordan redressed.

"Yes, Mr. Proctor?"

"Let's not mention these parts to anyone else yet. A lot has to be done on the backend to acquire new inventory such as this." He tapped his left leg, confident this brief exchange would squelch any possibility that Keith would give it a second thought once Jordan left the clinic.

"Yes, sir. I won't mention it. I'll email you the serials directly?"

"That would be splendid."

Jordan looked back at his top-of-the-line scooter as he stood in the doorway. "You know what to do with that, yes?"

"I'll call your driver and have him pick it up and return it to your residence. No worries."

"Hopefully, this will be the last time we have to wrestle the logistics this way for quite some time."

"Hopefully."

Jordan nodded to the receptionist on his way out. As he sauntered down the hallway, he slowed as he passed the physical therapy room, ever grateful he'd been rich enough from the start to avoid such a public display of weakness. All of his therapy had been done in the privacy of his Manhattan penthouse with top-of-the-line therapists.

In one corner, a slight-of-frame young physical therapist was helping a child with a missing right arm to strengthen his left one. In the opposite, a burly middle-aged trainer with muscles coming from his earlobes helped a young buck, who couldn't have been more than twenty-five, navigate the parallel bars like an elite gymnast missing both legs. The guy wore a military-green stringer that said *Go Army*.

Go Army, indeed. The Army ran off with both the man's legs.

No worries, though. On the first floor, an army of Blane Park therapists and psychiatrists took up halls of offices designed to allow amputees, trauma victims, disgruntled employees, and the occasional gambling addict to vent their frustrations and walk off with a happy new mental health skill to work on. Bruce's office was down there somewhere...

Strap on your new leg on the third floor.

Put on your big boy pants on the lobby level.

No thanks. Jordan was beyond *that* kind of therapy. All done with the "let it go" nonsense.

He should count his blessings that, though his trauma was legitimate, he didn't endure war—only a car wreck. And he still had one leg, after all.

But Jordan Proctor counted greenbacks, not blessings. For this, he forgave himself.

And soon, Proctor Alliance would infiltrate every aspect of Blane Park Medical with facilities that patients literally couldn't live without—and insurance companies couldn't refuse to pay for.

Affordable and efficient is how he'd sold the partnership to Underwood. Affordable and efficient wins elections—and makes the Jordan Proctors of the world rich.

He straightened his posture even more, testing out the balance of the new leg. Soon, Proctor would own Blane Park facilities around the nation.

And the pièce de résistance? The cherry on top that no one saw coming?

The mighty Craig Thompson had poked his head out of his own trauma stench to return to the ER bays. And Jordan would own him, too.

Right down to the tile in the man's bathroom backsplash.

10

Avenging or betraying?

Craig full-on believed that he was setting out to avenge Emma's tragic end, but handing over the keycards to Wagz to the twenty-something substitute dog groomer a week after Mel's folder derailed his life felt more like a betrayal.

Even more of a gut punch was that old Toby would be spending his days at Wagz with Rhett Duncan instead of Craig.

He had barely started his search for a new groomer when Rhett came across his radar, the well-connected realtor next door calling him with the lead. "Kid's new to the area. Mom's a hot shot with some legal firm. Daddy's rich. I put his parents into one of those new estate homes out in Landry Hills. Rhett's one of those spoiled adult-ish men who believes he can live off his online life-coaching jobs. Kudos to Mom and Dad for cutting him off. Maybe he'll grow a pair."

Craig's eyes widened, and Brian caught himself. "I know that's not very professional. Rhett's done some groomer training and his parents knew my office was next door to yours and... Well, they'd actually asked if you were hiring a while back. I figured if you were hiring, there'd have been a sign in the window."

"Don't worry about it. Glad for the referral. I need—" Craig hesitated, reaching for the right words. "I need to get back to the medical side of things before I start losing my hard-earned skillset. And my retirement cushion." Not a total lie, but not a total truth, either.

Brian chuckled. "Give Rhett a try, then. I'll pop in and check on things if you'd like. And when you're sick of paying rent..."

Craig chuckled at the plug Brian often jabbed him with. "Thanks, buddy." It'd be more likely that Hackett would kick up a ruckus if something other than Toby's presence was amiss next door. Brian and Hackett didn't have the typical master-dog relationship. Neither cared for the other, but they co-existed well so long as Brian never crossed Hackett's sense of duty.

And that shepherd carried a huge sense of duty.

Brian had come through in a big way—again. Wagz got a solid start in part due to the lineup of service dogs in the K-9 Unit Brian sent Craig's way. The spotlight in the Indy-Star with Officer Zoe Rigley and her bright-eyed Ava brought much-needed publicity, and Craig could give back to the community—something Emma would've loved.

Despite Rhett's cliched living arrangements, the kid was pleasantly above par. The dogs took to him. Toby brightened around him. Rhett had been trained well in whatever oddball grooming classes he'd taken. After a few intense days of one-on-one guidance, Craig finally placed the keycard to Wagz's state-of-the-art lock in Rhett's hands seven days after Melody had placed that old-school folder in Craig's. Craig was glad Toby had taken to the new groomer, and the dog didn't seem to mind when Craig told him to settle and left the shop without him.

Craig aimed his Jeep for Blane Park Medical to start a new old job.

Neither Craig nor Emma had ever had any trouble finding employment. Mount Lombard in Queens head-hunted them straight out of Johns Hopkins way before graduation. More than a dozen Level I trauma centers all along the Eastern seaboard and several in Indiana, including the fledgling Blane Park, practically fell over them, promising the moon. There was comfort in knowing as long as they kept their licensure and insurance, neither would ever have to worry about job security.

Craig wondered, given the national physician shortage, if Blane Park would be falling all over themselves to have him back on board, no matter how rusty his skills might be.

Compared to the skyscraper-locked land of Manhattan, Indianapolis was truly letting the hem out of the city. No second set of skyscrapers for Circle City, but sprawling medical and business complexes eating up farmland? That was another matter entirely.

The Blane Park campus welcomed its employees and patients with its logo—outstretched navy palms holding a red heart. Their logo was everywhere, and once a season, the logo danced above the Salesforce Tower building thanks to proprietary holographic tech. Branding meant big business, and apparently, Blane Park was all about the business side of things. Alfred Underwood, attention hog he was, ensured Blane spared no expense there.

Craig navigated the halls of his soon-to-be employer and

headed toward the Human Resources offices. He opened the frosted glass door, the aroma of coffee and vanilla greeted him. He gave his name to a worker-bee secretary, who stammered that he could wait for Linda. Blane Park Medical in blue letters shone from behind a waterfall installation on the wall opposite the opulent seating area. He slid into one of the three leather couches. Skylights above him let in the midday sun and warmed the waiting area.

The tiny, half-circle black cameras oversaw the whole area. The little dots on the walls above each office door and the jittery movements of the secretary seemed a stark contrast to the design's intended effect.

Craig didn't have to wait long before he was filling out employment paperwork in Linda's office, complete with acknowledgment of the receipt of the Blane Park Medical Mission Statement pages topped with the tagline—Where Patients Matter Most. Linda, a stern-looking woman with wire-rimmed glasses and a sweater cardigan in the same navy as the logo with an embroidered heart, looked over his shoulder far too often.

Craig was a Level I Trauma expert. Not to mention the proud owner of a dog grooming business. He didn't need help with a simple W2.

He vaguely remembered signing a mountain of documents with Emma at his side when they first hired on at Blane. He couldn't for the life of him remember seeing this fierce woman, though, and he didn't remember running into Mel—he and Emma would've been sure to have a long conversation about that if either of them had been aware that his former girlfriend was employed here.

Flipping through the stack of documents, Craig was glad he'd kept up with his main credentialling, but he'd had no privileges at any Indiana hospital for a couple of years.

He'd made it clear that he wanted nothing to do with ERs or trauma centers ever again, and the powers that be left him alone.

Now, waiting for Linda and her eagle eyes to ensure he'd dotted all his I's, he began to wonder if the always-short-staffed local medical community, specifically Blane Park, didn't leave him alone because of Emma. Because of what may have inadvertently led to her death...

If what Melody had pieced together had any weight to it, Craig believed he needed in-person access to Blane Park Medical. He wanted to get the feel of the place, the lay of the land back in his mind, and, most of all, rub shoulders with higher-ups.

Underwood included.

The only way to do that was to do the job he was once so good at.

As he sat across from Linda, Craig couldn't help but diagnose the odd way she held her left hand as a possible previous spinal cord injury and nearly asked her about it, but he put the reins on his ego. At the top of his game, he could diagnose a half dozen random issues on any of his trauma patients, in addition to treating the trauma. Diagnostics would've been his second specialty choice had it carried more of a rush. Or any rush at all.

"So, how long before your leave did you work in Indianapolis?"

Craig swallowed hard. Blood and protruding bones and arresting hearts on a ticking clock never phased him. Linda from HR was another story. And the answer was right there in his curriculum vitae. And his leave of absence was from right here at Blane Park. Was she trying to trip him up? Or was she peacocking her authority by asking already-answered questions?

The trap Underwood had set for Mel was ringing in his mind. Is Linda in on "it?" Whatever "it" might mean.

"About two years in the ER. Four years off duty."

She flipped through the stack of papers that constituted his previous employment file, comparing it to the stack he'd just created. "And I see you're now current on licensure and malpractice."

Craig was getting antsy. He kept imagining Melody walking into the Human Resources suite of offices any moment. He hadn't spoken with her much since that night at the restaurant, only to say that he'd decided to hire an employee for Wagz and return to the ER part-time. He and Mel would not use Blane phone systems to communicate, nor the Blane-supplied email system. "This call may be recorded for quality purposes and training" sounded off like a mantra at the beginning of most phone calls. Craig didn't want to take a chance that it was actually true.

Instead, Mel and Craig decided to rendezvous once a week at The Sicilian. It was further for Mel to Uber, but most Blane Park employees lived nearer to the main campus than Bella Square, and it was a reasonably quiet little spot. And they'd play it pro at work should they happen to run into each other. His time in the HR department would be the biggest risk of that since Mel had no reason to be in the trauma bays once Craig started his shifts.

Mel assured him she would be in and out of budget meetings all week. He prayed she'd lay low and not take any more documents, privileged or not. Until he knew if they had anything to take to the authorities, it was best she stay clear of any more suspicion.

Linda was still rattling on. "—badge ready tomorrow after we clear it with the security team. Someone here will take your photo and get you set up with your lanyard. You'll report to the head of Emergency Services, Dr. McTilde. You might recognize that name. He was here before you quit—I mean before you took leave."

Recognize the name? That was the understatement of the century.

Aside from being competitive classmates in high school, Craig had ended up with seniority of career over the man at Mount Lombard. Because anywhere he and Emma went, Eli had to go too.

Craig signed up for basketball his freshman year of high school. Eli did too.

Craig joined and then quit the debate team. Eli followed suit. Always tagging along. Always trying to one-up Craig.

It didn't change when Eli and Craig became fully formed adult males, either. In fact, things seemed to get worse.

Eli McTilde was a generally competent physician, all things being equal, but had become bitter when the higher-ups knighted Craig as Trauma team leader at Mount Lombard, forcing Eli to take a lower rung in the pecking order. Craig, as he'd done in high school, mostly ignored Eli in the emergency room atmosphere unless patient care depended on their communication.

"I'm familiar with Dr. McTilde. I'm thrilled to be a part of the team." Eli would be thrilled to be Craig's senior supervisor now.

As Craig stood to leave Linda to her duties, she looked at him over her glasses. "Be careful in that department, Dr. Thompson. You know how crazy things can get in the trauma bays." A small shiver went down his spine. This woman was an oblivious, overbearing hen—or she was sending him a stern warning.

Likely, she was an overworked, bitter soul who had no life outside OSHA, HIPAA, and 401(k)s. He couldn't help but wonder if Melody would tread down the same path if she didn't get out of this job—or at least out of this company.

On his way out of the human resources suite, he willed himself to keep his head down and not acknowledge the eyes in the sky. He ran right into the firm frame of an oncoming human—and the mop bucket he was pushing down the hall.

"Dr. Thompson?"

Craig looked up, embarrassed by the hurried escape from the HR Courtyard.

"Trevor?"

The guy was one of Craig's favorite employees in all of Blane. Emma had adored him. Trevor frequently worked double shifts and ran circles around most folks twenty years his junior. He'd do anything the maintenance department needed only stopping short at direct patient care. Mop. Fix. Haul. Lug. And he made it happen and did so in a way that lifted your spirits. "That's not in my job description" wasn't in Trevor's vocabulary.

"I'm sure glad to see you back. You comin' back, ain't ya?"

"Yes, sir. You're still going strong, I see."

Trevor's usually jovial face clouded as he toyed with his name badge. "I suppose so."

Craig knew better. In the four years since he'd seen Navy Vet turned maintenance man, Trevor had aged significantly. Craig couldn't believe the guy was still upright, let alone working. "Hope to see you around, Trevor."

"I'm sure you will. When you startin'?"

"In a week or so. Two weeks at the latest."

"I'll be around. They're always runnin' short in the

support departments. Maybe see ya 'round—if it's first shift."

"Yup. Starting on first. Back... back in the ER." Craig cleared his throat.

Trevor hung his head again and fiddled with the mop handle. "So, so sorry about Emma. When I'm back in those bays—"

Craig saved him from the awkward condolence and forced a smile. "It's okay. It's time to move on. It's what Emma would've wanted."

"She was sure somethin'." Trevor straightened his posture and met Craig's gaze. "She's surely missed."

"Yes, sir."

"A couple of weeks, then?" Trevor nodded and looked up at the half-sphere keeping watch over the hallway. Craig tried not to read too much into that, but he couldn't help it. Hypervigilance had him paying attention to details he would've never noticed before. Lest he should have a "trip and fall."

"We'll grab a quick lunch one day." Trevor smiled and went on his way. Craig headed to the parking lot, nearly bumping into a well-dressed man with a slight limp. Craig apologized and went on, happy to be in the crisp fresh air and more than ready to rescue Toby from Rhett—or Rhett from Toby, should that be the case.

But Craig couldn't stop himself from pausing to look over his shoulder as the man in the suit approached the side entrance. That limp. A knee injury? No...

As the man swung the door open, the breeze picked up enough to wrap the pant leg tight along his side. Ahh. The gentleman had an amputation. He must've had quite the high-end physical therapy regimen. His limp was barely noticeable.

11

Melody's head spun as she left the conference room and pushed the down button on the elevator. The never-ending butt-kissing Blane Park does with Proctor Alliance was wearying to the soul way before she found the thread between them and Proctor's faulty supplies and software.

Now? It was migraine-inducing. The week's never-ending budget meetings would be exhausting no matter what else was going on—and a lot was going on.

Enter the question of whether to speak up about all the new purchases and fundraisers. Why is no one going through the proper channels?

She adjusted her lanyard and toyed with her security badge. Her photo was a bit outdated. Her hair in the picture was past her shoulders; now it's at the bottom of her earlobes. She ditched the hunter-green glasses in favor of contacts, at least when she was in public. Her eyes had been in a constant state of puffy and dark since she stood in front of Linda two years ago for her Blane Park mugshot.

As the elevator doors swung open and she rounded the corner toward HR, Craig Thompson was leaving the offices, his head down. She froze in her tracks as he turned away without noticing she'd exited the elevator.

Thankfully, Trevor had come around the corner, engaging Craig in conversation. Craig was none the wiser that she was within mere feet of him. Mel exhaled hard, not realizing she'd been holding her breath. Running smack into him in the office would've been bad. Cameras aside, she wouldn't have been able to control her flushed cheeks and stammering tongue should Craig have acknowledged her.

Melody made her way to her office, careful to keep her head level and unassuming when she passed the entryway camera. She couldn't help but wonder if the eyes in the sky were honed in on her every microexpression. She left her frosted glass door ajar so she could hear incoming problems and avoid being snuck up on. Behind the safety of her work-station, she breathed deep, held it for a four-count, and controlled the exhale. Just like Dr. Tanberg taught her, his soothing voice counting off the seconds in her head.

She shouldn't be worried about someone seeing her and Craig rubbing shoulders in passing. No one at Blane Park knew her well. She wouldn't let anyone get too close in any arena of her life after Craig dumped her. This went doubly so for past and current coworkers. As far as she knew, no one at Blane Park was aware—or at least, they hadn't cared —they'd been a part of each other's lives. It was high school, after all. She supposed anyone with a Ben Davis yearbook, or the dozens of other Ben Davis graduates employed there, could catch black-and-white glimpses of the pair together in various extracurricular high school activities. Still, she doubted anyone cared enough about her to bother being nosy.

It was ancient history.

Melody was happy to be uber-private and on her own.

At least that's what she'd been telling herself—and Dr. Tanberg—for years.

"You're never alone, Mel. You've got me."

Even though he'd gifted her with a private number, she believed Doc Tanberg had a skewed idea of "you've got me." *Yes, Doc. So long as I pay my therapy bill.*

She scooted up to her desk and opened random files on her screen, not caring to see anything in particular. She avoided opening any new hire files, knowing that soon enough, she'd have to process Dr. Craig Thompson's paperwork.

Shortly after their breakup, Melody endured unkind jabs from her friends. "She's an un-Craiged Melody," a jab on the Righteous Brothers song. Along with "Bet you won't watch *Ghost* anymore," she'd had enough of letting even her closest girlfriends know what was going on in her life.

Being un-Craiged led to her being unhinged for most of college, getting a rather late start on that endeavor. She'd stayed local. Once a Hoosier, always a Hoosier, graduating from Indiana University.

She'll take her hard-earned degree, her cat, the piles of books, and the paycheck from Blane Park for as long as she has a job here.

But if Craig finds validation for any of her sleuthing, those paychecks may evaporate.

"Hey, Mel. Did you see the hunk of a new hire that strode out of here?" the office secretary, Carol, jibed.

Melody shook her head no and scootched a little closer to her screen. Pictures of Omega dotted the edges of her monitor. The floofy gray feline posed on top of every surface she wasn't allowed to be on all over Mel's house. Omega owned the place.

"Man, Mel. How did you miss that guy? He takes up the whole room. If I wasn't married—"

"Yeah, but you are. Let's not start a potential sexual harassment lawsuit. You did say *new hire*, right?"

Carol blushed and went back to her stack of files. "I was just sayin'..."

Linda, the hound dog of Human Resources, came across what the HR ladies dubbed the Courtyard, a waiting area connecting the suite of management offices, complete with an industrial-style Keurig station, mini-fridge, and waterworks wall decor. Blane Park spared no expense for its employees.

"Melody, here's the start of Dr. Thompson's file. See that his is processed before anyone else's. He'll be starting in the ER sooner than he realizes. McTilde said they're short again this week." Linda handed her a stack of files, Craig's on the top. "Everyone in that stack will need updated tax forms and confidentiality agreements."

"This week?" Mel couldn't hide her surprise.

"Yes, Mel. This week. We're short-staffed back there. As always."

Mel smiled and took the files from the lady's wrinkled hands. Linda was five years past due for retirement, at least. Mel may throw herself a party when Linda finally retires. Take one of her me-days and stay indoors reading with Omega.

Melody typed in the ID number from Craig's folder into the computer. The thought of photographing Craig against the blue backdrop that always hung in her office corner made her wipe her hands on her slacks. She started processing the file, inputting all the most intimate digital information on a person one could into various fields on the Blane Park server. Social Security, bank information, retirement plan funds. She tried to imagine what it would be like for Craig on his first day back.

Then her heart sank.

The plaque.

In the very trauma bay where Emma died.

Would it trigger him? Hinder his work?

Oh no... what have I done? When she and Trevor had hung it, never in a million years would she have thought that Craig would ever work in any Blane Park facility again, let alone where—

"Oh, I forgot to tell you," Linda turned back to Melody. "We're getting a new machine to code the security badges. It should arrive tomorrow afternoon. Proctor Alliance is sending a courier delivery."

"What's wrong with the badge system we've got now?" You'd think something so major would've been brought up in the budget meeting. Another item to add to her ever-growing mental list of "Am I nuts, or am I being left out on purpose?" Both?

With her Master's degree, she was more than qualified to handle all aspects of human resource issues, but the Blane culture? Even those with five fewer seconds of experience treated her as an underling.

"They won't match, I guess. We'll be slammed redoing the entire staff's badges—" Linda left Melody's office before she even finished her sentence, rattling on about how salaried folks don't get paid enough to stay after hours to update badges. How the shredder machines will be working overtime destroying the old badges and what a waste—

"Match what?" Mel called after her, but it was Carol who bopped her head in the doorway before Linda's menthol aroma had dissipated. "Yeah, they won't match the keyfobs." Carol rolled her eyes toward Linda's trail. "All new lock systems. You remember how badly these updates went last time? Now we're doing both at the same time. This week is already a nightmare, and it's only Monday."

"Why wasn't I told of this sooner?" Mel's head spun. She was *just* in the budget meeting. This had to be a huge expense.

"Linda said Underwood and that guy from Proctor were here last week. She forgot to mention it to me too." Carol shrugged.

Linda never forgot anything.

Proctor Alliance will now hold the keys—literally and digitally—to Blane Park Medical's kingdom, any property Proctor Alliance owned, Blane Park or not.

Mel swallowed hard. Unlike Linda, Melody would likely not survive her human resources position long enough for anyone to wish her wrinkled carcass would hurry up and retire already.

12

THOUGH THE SUN wasn't quite up yet, Craig dropped his Ray-Bans over his tired eyes and slid into the driver's seat of his Jeep after dropping Toby off at Wagz. It'd taken some doing to get any real sleep last night after two odd phone calls, first Eli then with Mel... He couldn't think about that right now. It was going to be a long enough day.

The Jeep was Emma's choice—something neither had ever dreamed of owning when they were pounding pavement on sunny days and catching ride shares back and forth from their loft in Queens to Mount Lombard. Something so ostentatiously gas-guzzling would have been frowned upon for more than one reason—and they'd have to pick up extra shifts to pay the parking fees. Their "adrenaline downsizing," as his late wife put it, would require a vehicle, and she wanted something substantial to handle the snowy roads — and the Indiana deer population — lest they end up trauma patients themselves.

He tugged at the collar of his scrub shirt and slid his hand into the empty seat. He and Emma had worked as many of the same shifts as possible, and he always drove. Toby had since occupied the passenger seat, his substantial Labrador girth causing Craig to keep the seatbelt perpetually buckled so the alarm wouldn't nag him to death. But today, on his first day back to the ER in four years, Craig allowed his hand to rest in the passenger seat just as he did the dreadful night that Emma didn't make the ride home with him to their bungalow in Bella Square.

Resting his head back on the headrest, he allowed the images to flood his mind. He knew they would come at some point, and he might as well give them the room to do their nasty work before he started his shift an *entire week* before he was really ready to.

The ink wasn't even dry on his signatures from yesterday.

Deep breath. Fifteen years together, five of them married, and one bullet takes it all away in the blink of an eye...

Blane Park was slammed that night. Every glass-encased trauma bay and curtained triage room was occupied—or about to be. Craig was in director mode, that soaring surge of adrenaline propelling him through like so many shifts in NYC. The Indianapolis hospital could go from zero to a hundred in a heartbeat, like any ER, but he'd never seen it like Mount Lombard—never zero and always surging at a strong two hundred. That night, Craig assigned teams to bays and patients to teams as car wrecks and heart attacks and strokes streamed through the doors faster than the Midwest staff was accompanied to. Still, each team member treated each patient as if they were the only one in the building.

Every life mattered and every second counted.

It was one of those shifts where the ambulance bay doors remained open more than they stayed vacuumed-sealed shut, and no one had time to pay attention to that small detail.

Matt was on security that night, stationed at those doors. Laurie, his partner, floated the halls of the trauma center, and Edward hung at the patient's ambulatory entrance. Bay four needed an extra pair of arms for an overdose patient, so Laurie swung over to cover the ambulance bay, and Matt lent his help with restraining the patient. All hands on deck.

Emma and her team were in bay two with a little boy from the east side who'd been hit by a dump truck while riding his bike across Washington Street. Emma had rolled her eyes when the EMTs gave report. What was an eight-year-old doing crossing Washington alone on a bike? Compound fractures of the humerus. Unknown head trauma. Unknown internal issues. They were waiting behind a car crash victim for the MRI suite to free up.

Funny, Craig thought as he massaged his temple. Any other night, no matter how slammed or how slow, the details would've been lost on him after some time, definitely after four years. Craig could see dozens of patients a day, six days a week. Though his memory served him well enough to put off dictating his reports until the end of shift, or perhaps even the end of the week, afterward, he cleared the mental slate to make room for the next wave.

But that little boy, Joel, he would not forget.

He would not forget the way Emma brushed Craig's cheek in passing after she'd stabilized the child, a gesture she'd done a thousand times both in NYC and Indy. It used to garner suspicious looks from the staff, but once folks realized how dedicated the two docs were to each other, it became part of the culture of working with the Thompsons. And Craig leaned in to her touch every time.

Sitting in the Jeep, he removed his hand from her empty seat and felt his own cheek, trying to resurrect the sensation. It wasn't the same. No butterflies. No rush. The only thing on his face was the deceptive warmth of the November sun shining through the windshield. He knew outside the confines of the vehicle, the wind was brisk and the temps were near the freezing mark.

That brush, though. That was the last touch she'd share with him before all hell broke loose. At first, Craig didn't know where the gunman had entered. He'd assumed the ambulance bay, given that those doors had remained open all night, and with the ongoing chaos, anyone dressed in similar colors as the first responders could waltz right in. Later, he'd learn it was through the walk-in patient entrance. With all the navy blue-clad EMTs coming and going, no one had noticed the navy-blue-clad mentally disturbed white male, 6'2", newly widowed, handgun tucked inside his jacket.

That night, a receptionist stationed outside the ambulatory entrance buzzed in a lab tech and then turned her attention to the switchboard, which had lit up like a Christmas tree. The man had walked in behind the tech as if he belonged there.

The radiology techs running down the hall inside the ER ran right past him. The charge nurse was away from her station, and he walked past the desk into the central hub. Everyone was doing their jobs, no one saw.

The high-tech weapons detection system guarding the exterior patient entrance didn't pick him up either. If it had, the receptionist would've flipped a switch, and the place would've gone on lockdown. Even if she'd been slow on the draw, the system alert would've handed the guards precious seconds to react, maybe not by the first bullet, but definitely before the rain of them started in the middle of the bays.

Matt, Laurie, and Edward reacted once the shot was fired, but none of the three had a chance to react any sooner. Laurie was knocked in the head with a quick whack of the gunman's weapon but managed to draw on the man. Her line of fire was directly into the main hub, where a dozen staff and a few patients were gathered. "GUN, GUN. Stop, drop your weapon!" Craig and Emma turned on their heels and ducked low, their deeply ingrained active shooter training from Mount Lombard kicking in.

Laurie's head dripped blood, and Craig went toward her, but she shook him away, pointing in the direction of the gunman — who was headed toward the bay where Emma's small patient lay on the gurney.

Before Craig could turn on his heels again, he followed Emma's gaze after the man, and before Craig could utter a syllable, Emma bolted for Joel's bay, standing broadside in front of the boy.

"Stop, sir. We can work this out, please put the gun—"

The next moments unfolded in slow motion, each second an eternity, and every one of them headed for only one outcome.

The wiry man held his weapon, barrel down, the piece shaking in his right hand. Craig uncemented his feet from in front of Laurie and made five or six long strides toward the man.

Matt and Edward appeared, flanking the gunman, their weapons raised, shouting commands.

Staff scattered to secure patient bays and lock down the emergency room.

The shaking man took a step.

Craig took another stride.

Emma backed into the bay. The man used his left hand to steady the weapon. She looked wide-eyed at Craig over the man's shoulder.

"No, Emma! No!"

But Craig knew. Fifteen years of glances and brushes and reading the woman he loved. He *knew*.

And he knew that Emma knew, too.

Emma threw herself over the boy who screamed out in agony—his fresh fractures no doubt seething under Emma's weight. She ignored the wails and curled her body over the boy as tightly as she could. The first shot hit low, connecting with the metal frame of the hospital bed. The second shattered the glass between Joel's bay and the next.

Screams all around. Craig took two more steps.

Matt fired and missed, the bullet skittering down the corridor and connecting with a mobile computer stand, sparks flying. Edward and Laurie advanced quickly, but neither could risk a shot into the congested ER.

The man squeezed off a third shot, and Emma's tightly curled frame relaxed. Another shot. Another.

Craig and Ed tackled the man to the ground, and all that was left was the weeping.

Brian Rivers pulled into the spot next to him, and Craig let out the breath he'd been holding in—likely had held it the whole time he recalled the incident. Hackett was hanging his head out the window, drool running down the side of Brian's car.

Craig nodded at the realtor, and despite the sunglasses, winced at the first rays of morning light. He started the engine and cracked a window, letting the crisp air help bring him back to the present. "Morning, Brian." Craig's voice was shaky.

"Morning Cr—Hackett-no. Come back!" The ex-police dog had no intention of doing anything Brian asked. No way Brian was going to reign in the K9 if the dog didn't choose to be reigned in—much like the trauma memories from the shooting—a rogue dog on the loose. As soon as Craig had comprehended the contents of that folder, those memories unleashed in painful detail.

And now again, after reinstating his position at Blane.

Craig waved goodbye to a frazzled Brian and pulled the Jeep out of the parking lot. He thought he'd have a week to process and hoped he'd given himself adequate time in the parking lot behind Wagz to bring them to the surface, acknowledge them once again, and tamp them down to be able to function.

Only time would tell.

As he drove to Blane Park, he wondered how much of the ER would have been upgraded since the shooting. Shatterproof glass? Revamping staff protocols? Tall, strong metal detectors that would actually detect metal instead of the discreet, sleek Proctor Alliance "weapons detection" system that had failed at least three times now? Did they just patch the bug in the Proctor software? Maybe partner with a firm whose sole focus is protecting people instead of one that also supplies cafeteria napkins.

Proctor. Too many irons in too many fires.

Craig supposed he'd find out soon enough.

Because in about an hour, Dr. Craig Thompson would take his first shift in four years in the very department where his wife died a hero.

He flicked on the Jeep's wipers. It was starting to snow. The first one of the season.

Emma loved the snow...

13

Mel loved the snow.

The overcast sky spat out the first twirly flakes of the season. Normally, Melody would seize the opportunity to burn a sick day or a vacation day and stay in front of the fire. Even if there were only five flakes, this was her chosen way to take a "me day" and reset. Sometimes, she'd take two or three. Her vacation didn't roll over year to year, and any time away from Linda and the hustle of the HR Courtyard was a good time.

A book.

A blanket.

Omega—if Omega would grace Melody with the gift of his feline companionship.

But today wasn't about her or her wishes. Today was Craig's first day back at Blane Park.

Craig had called late last night—it was going on midnight. She got word of his earlier-than-expected start date before he had, but she'd let him ask questions and ramble on. It was the least she could do after taping that passive-aggressive note to Wagz's back door.

Passive aggressive being the term Dr. T. labeled it when she aired the event out over a quick texting session. Mel had always carried a great deal of guilt over some of her choices, but adding in new-to-her behavior, aka turning herself into a proverbial sheriff nailing up condemned notices to dilapidated properties, was way out of line.

"I start in the morning. I'm to report to HR first for a temporary ID or something?"

Mel stammered all over that phone call. "Yeah. I, uh. Yeah. We're getting a new badge striper. But yeah, come to the Courtyard, and I'll see that you get what you need."

"Hey, I'm sorry. It sounds like I woke you up—"

"No, no." He had, actually. Woken her up and nearly gave her a heart attack. But she was sure she'd have sounded like a barely-awake human had he called at four p.m.

"Mel. There's something else."

"What?" Mel's heart had sunk to her stomach at the tone in Craig's voice.

"McTilde called me. Asked if I'd caught up with you yet. Made it a point to comment on working with an old flame. His old flame, too, by the way, not to mention mine."

With that, her heart went to her toes, and a fiery embarrassment stung her cheeks. She should've told him. She should've disclosed that relationship with Eli—however brief it may have been.

"Mel?"

"Yeah. I mean. There are lots of Ben Davis grads working at Blane. A few of them are bound to know about us. I mean you and me. But mostly they know about—"

"You and Eli. Well, I wanted to give you a heads-up. But, let's stick with the plan. Keep it casual." Craig cut her off. He had a knack for that kind of grace. Not allowing folks to stumble over their well-meaning words.

She should've been the one to give Craig a heads-up... Ugg. How many more ways can she mess things up?

She'd stayed awake worrying until a fitful sleep overcame her around two a.m. Not much energy to go on before facing Craig—and the jeering Eli.

Some personalities never mature past those high school years. Eli was one of them. Competitive. Whiny. Always one step behind everyone he wanted to outperform. Why he didn't stay in NYC was beyond her. Why come back where everyone knew you were second to the Thompsons? Heck, even Mel had out-schooled him on occasion.

She was ever so grateful to have not let things go too far between them. She couldn't imagine what kind of junk Eli would hold over her if she had.

Mel dumped the last few sips of her second cup of coffee down the drain and rinsed the mug. Omega skittered up in front of her, a tuft of gray fur escaped from his frame and floated mid-air. She grabbed it with one hand and put it in the trash. "Not on the counter, you." She moved the cat to the floor. "Not that you won't go right back up there when I turn around."

Omega did just that. Butt in the air, head in the sink, lapping watered-down coffee splashes. Mel grabbed him a little more firmly and set him on the floor, but not before he reached around and gifted her with a new scratch across the top of her right hand.

"You're the devil, Omega." A devil she adored and loathed simultaneously, especially when he drew blood. She washed and rinsed off the scratch in the sink, did a better job of rinsing out the coffee remains, and leaned on the counter, head in her hands.

Things were moving fast. She'd almost rather be in another migraine-inducing budget meeting two floors above the Courtyard. Delegate the security badge task to Carol—or heaven forbid, Linda could do it, though her demeanor with most of the staff directly contradicted the Caring Hands branding.

Then another thought skidded full stop in her mind. Proctor's new machine was coming, what was it, this afternoon? Craig would need his badge to work as soon as he hit the ER department. He couldn't wait until noon. The badges gave access to important parts of the ER, and patient safety dictated that all employees be identifiable at all times —especially ones that held literal lives in their hands.

Which meant she'd have to see Craig. Twice. Once for the temp badge and once again for the updated one once Proctor's machine was up and running.

Two badges.

In one day.

A crash from behind startled her upright. Omega, on the counter opposite, had knocked off a coffee cup. Mel's favorite—one of a pair she'd picked up on vacation to Colorado that she displayed on the counter.

"Omega!" Mel tucked Omega under her arm, and like a switch was flipped, Omega started purring and rubbing his face on Mel's shirt—which she'd now have to change because no lint roller could tackle the amount of hair he was gifting her.

"How much caffeine? Huh? And I suppose you chased that down with a hit of catnip?"

She dropped him on the couch and tossed him a new mouse toy to keep him occupied while she cleaned up the shards of her coffee mug. It wasn't too bad. The mug had broken into three parts, two parts cup, one part handle. If it could be glued, it would never hold liquid again.

She tried to arrange the pieces to see if it could be done,

even for appearance's sake. She precariously held the three parts together next to the unbroken mug.

Two mugs side by side. Anyone with eyes could clearly tell one wasn't right.

Two badges side by side, and maybe, someone with the right set of eyes could spot the one that wouldn't hold liquid...

Omega was rolling his entire body all over the toy, then stopped to look at Mel with those coal-black eyes. "I get it. You're a genius. An evil one, but a genius."

Mel changed her blouse and gave Omega a head scratch on her way out the door.

Since hospital policy requires old security badges to be surrendered when new ones are issued, she had the ride into work to figure out how to confiscate Dr. Craig Thompson's morning badge when he came in for his new one this afternoon, making seeing Craig twice in one day not such a bad thing.

A simple sleight of hand out of the line of sight of the cameras. Mel wished she'd paid more attention when her cousin had tried to teach her magic tricks in fifth grade.

Dr. T. did say she should take more bold moves in her life, hadn't he?

And just like that, Mel forgot all about the memorial plaque in trauma bay three.

14

Craig tried not to fidget with his scrubs, or his hair still damp with the snow, or his scruff that he'd not bothered to shave off this morning. He stood in front of Melody Atkins, vice president of HR, and tried to smile professionally. He'd lost track of the early morning buffer he'd given himself after Emma's last day washed over him.

He shifted his weight from one foot to the other. He'd wanted to feel in control for his first shift. He'd wanted more days at Wagz, ensuring that Rhett actually had things under control.

He'd wanted a clean shave, too.

But here he was, scruff and all. Rushing. Disheveled. Hoping not to let his apathy for McTilde seep out of every pore the second he saw the man in the trauma bays.

Hoping to connect the rest of the dots for Mel.

Wait. Not for Mel. For Emma. He had to remember that...

Breathe.

"I'm sorry, Dr. Thompson, for all these extra steps. But we're updating our security system this afternoon, and you'll need access to ER doors and other electronics way before two p.m. Dr. McTilde wants you to hit the ground running."

Melody had already told him this last night. Her sing-song dialogue now was for the sake of show for Carol, who kept poking her head in Mel's office for one reason or another. There were a few more forms to sign and the security badge to create. Craig had planned to take care of this a whole day before his original start date—not in the minutes before start of shift.

"Well, we can't disappoint—" Craig almost said Eli, but formalities abound on Day One. "Dr. McTilde." He shook his head, remembering not to be too familiar with anyone here, despite his classmate connection. Despite just discovering Mel and Eli had a fling of sorts—and not too long ago in the grand scope of things. He had a job to do: Patients first, digging second—and reconnecting wasn't in the triage plan.

"It's no problem. I understand." He tried another smile, and Mel snapped the camera button. Spots of green and blue danced in the periphery of his vision from the flash. The badge maker whirled to life, and in a few short seconds, Mel handed him a still-warm ID card, complete with a blue and white lanyard printed with Blane Park Medical alternating with the Caring Hands logo over and over.

As if he needed a reminder of where he was.

Craig rubbed his eyes to clear the remaining flash blindness. "Thank you for your time, Miss Atkins."

"You're welcome, Doctor. And welcome back." She smiled at him. If they'd never met before, Emma or not, in that second, Craig would've noticed the kindness in her hazel eyes. A stark contrast to Carol's hungry blue ones and Linda's overworked and underpaid browns. She broke his gaze and turned her back to him, fussing with something on her desk. "I'll let you know when I need you back in here for the upgraded badge this afternoon. I might be able to use this photo on the new system. If I can get away from the soon-to-be long lines, I'll hand-deliver it, and you won't have to leave your patients in the ER."

Craig smiled and nodded. Instead of prolonging the awkwardness, he backed out of Mel's office and spun on his heels in the Courtyard—nearly running chest-to-chest into Alfred Underwood.

"Craig! I was hoping to catch you down here." Mr. Underwood hadn't changed since he'd first welcomed Craig and Emma to the Blane Park Medical "family" years ago. Taller than Craig by an inch but fifty pounds lighter, Mr. Underwood made up for his thin frame with a deep baritone voice that could've been used to significant gain in the audiobook world—if the genre were dystopian and all is doomed.

"Mr. Underwood. Great to see you." Craig forced a smile. He was doing that a lot lately.

"I hope our great Human Resources team hasn't been giving you any grief. Linda keeps this place running top-notch, but she can be, well," He leaned in close. "Linda needs a vacation if you ask me."

"Everyone's been very welcoming. I'm glad to be back."

"Glad to hear it, glad to hear it." Underwood pounded on Craig's shoulder. Craig took a small step back, then checked himself. "How's the new business venture?"

Craig assumed he was talking about Wagz. "Great. It was Emma's passion project and I'm happy to see it through." It was a rehearsed line. Something he'd worked out that night Mel had posted the notice on his door. This was the first time the sentence fell out of his mouth, and it felt... off.

"Good, good. Hopefully you'll be all-in here at Blane and won't need to carry that silly burden much longer."

Craig had *not* practiced a response to such a blatant opinion of his business. Images rushed in of his graying Toby curled on his bed at Wagz and Diane's stupid Winston bulldog covered in pink goo and Max in the bath. The photo of Emma in her wedding dress hanging over the light switch.

Wagz's keys in Rhett's hands.

Craig's urge was to ball up his fist and punch Underwood in the throat, but before he could even respond civilly, Underwood mock-punched Craig in the stomach and turned with him down the hall. Underwood looked over his shoulder back into the Courtyard and up and down the hallway, then he looked Craig square in the face and held his gaze.

Craig's skin began to crawl, and he tried his best to keep eye contact with the CEO and not look up at the half-moon cameras above the Courtyard's entrance.

After what seemed like an awkward eternity, Underwood leaned in closer and finally spoke. "I need a fresh pair of eyes. You've been through it lately, and being back here has to be hard for you." He paused again, and Craig's pulse quickened. "But over the next few months, I'd like a report on how you think Dr. McTilde is running my Emergency Department. I believe the nursing team is afraid to tell me the truth. Between you and me, I think he's losing his edge."

Craig lost control of his eyebrows, which crept up toward his hairline. He unballed his fist at the request. He couldn't believe what Underwood was asking. "Sir, there are protocols in place for peer reviews and formal assessment—"

"Sure, sure. But you and I know those aren't always accurate. McTilde has a... way with the staff, and I'd like a competent opinion from someone more... more his equal than his subordinate."

"I *am* his subordinate."

"Sure, sure. But this is, well. Off the record." He slapped Craig's back again. "I'll catch up with you soon, Dr. Thompson. It sure is good to have you back." With that, the fearless Blane Park CEO turned for the elevators and took his all-is-doomed voice with him.

Craig's mind whirled.

McTilde a force? Emma had been a force, McTilde was always a semi-competent joke. And since when can't Alfred Underwood, the head of the whole Blane Park family, use his god-given spine and sit McTilde down for a chat if something was off?

Breathe. Remember your training.

Rat on McTilde: *Delayed.* He had to figure out if Underwood could be trusted, let alone confided in about a supervisor's competency. Craig had never seen this level of unprofessionalism across the board—and from one of the nation's most up-and-coming medical names. And though sticking it to Eli would feel better than good, Craig had always gone through proper channels to report another employee's conduct and had never stooped to the level of behind-the-scenes work Alfred was asking for.

Play it cool with Mel: *Urgent.* That McTilde was already jibing him about it was not a good sign. Craig needed to keep his wits about him.

Learn how to take foolish comments about Emma. And

Wagz. One that doesn't include a fist-balling reaction: *Urgent.*

Survive the first shift in the emergency room: *Immediate.* He needed to allow himself to revel in the thrill of the job. Of taking a patient from the brink of death and pouring hope into the situation. The emergency room was Craig's one-time comfort zone—he needed it to be that again. To keep him distracted from Toby's pouting image. From the folder's contents splayed on his wall. From Mel.

And from Emma's ghost.

15

Jᴏʀᴅᴀɴ Pʀᴏᴄᴛᴏʀ never drove in the snow, and if he weren't such a workaholic, he'd never ride in it either. Given his station, his lackeys could be dispatched wherever he needed them, allowing him to remain in the happy confines of his penthouse. But the meetings at Blane Park couldn't be pushed off another day—he'd already pushed them yesterday because he needed the time with Keith to update his prosthesis.

Today, though? Craig Thompson was the issue on the table, and no lackey could replace Jordan's eyes and ears in the meeting. Not to mention the hot-off-the-press text that lit his phone up from Bruce. The man's finally earning his wheels.

McTilde promised he'd have the champion ER doc in the bays for the duration of the daylight hours. Hopefully, he'll earn his wheels this week, too.

"Mind the others. They've forgotten, you know." Jordan always gave his personal drivers this stern warning every year—no matter whether he was riding with Edward in Manhattan or Nate here the Midwest. "Even the old-timers forget how to drive in the snow. Or folks think it sticks before it really does. Like now."

Jordan had to eat those words. Over the last twelve hours, the temperature had dropped and there was, indeed, enough precipitation to create a sheen on the roadways. The road crews hadn't foreseen this blast of pre-winter excitement, and a Saab side-wound its way into a fire hydrant on Michigan Avenue. Gushes of water sprayed the side of Jordan's SUV. Nate swerved hard to avoid the spray, and the Saab skidded a little, course-correcting seconds before fender-bending the vehicle ahead of them.

"For crying out loud." Jordan reached for his prosthetic, making sure the leg was still firmly attached after the jostling. It was. Quality parts, and all.

"Sorry, Sir. You okay back there?" Nate's eyes were wide in the rearview mirror.

"I'm fine. Just drive," Jordan snapped back as he reached forward to slide the privacy divider closed.

But Jordan was not fine. As he rubbed the synthetic leg, a bead of sweat started at the nape of his neck, working its way around to his forehead.

Jordan despised sweating. It showed weakness. He had the leg for that, though most people didn't notice that at first glance. But sweat? Shakes?

He was glad that the slowed traffic would allow him an extra quarter-hour to calm his nerves.

Chiding himself was not a characteristic Jordan allowed, for that trait would get him nowhere. Instead, Jordan forgave himself. Many people would be in fender-benders or slide-offs today. But Jordan experienced the worst of the worst in the realm of car crashes eight years ago.

MVAs, they call them in the emergency rooms.

Motor vehicle accidents.

Though his was no accident.

And it didn't happen because of the weather. It had been an August heat that rivaled that of the Sahara, mirage waves hovering over the concrete of the roadway like ghosts.

The wreck eight years ago happened because of jealousy. And rage.

He'd lost his wife.

His best friend.

His leg.

Of the three, he probably missed the leg the most. His leg never cheated on him, after all. If anyone had bothered taking a second look at the accident, Jordan Proctor would never have had the chance to create Proctor Alliance. Jordan Proctor would have made all kinds of other alliances, likely in Sing Sing.

Then to be declared not worthy of saving when compared with another. Imagine that. A full-grown male capable of work and paying taxes pushed aside for a child who could do nothing but suck her thumb and resources.

He would be forever grateful to Dr. Eli McTilde. Another soul who understood what it was like to be treated as a sub-par human. He would forgive McTilde the rookie errors he'd made in the ER that day. Errors that did not save his leg entirely, but at least have given him that much more of a stump to work with.

He would not—could not—forgive the elite Dr. Craig Thompson who most certainly possessed better-honed skills that would've allowed Jordan to walk the earth as a whole man. But the little girl with the burns had come first. Her skin deemed more valuable than his limb.

As Blane Park's silhouette peaked through a burst of flurries, a little bile came up in the back of his throat. He swallowed it down. He straightened, checking the hooks and anchors of his prosthesis once more. It was all Jordan could do yesterday not to shoulder-check the man outside Blane's HR entrance. Craig never gave Jordan a second glance—let alone a second chance.

He dug out his handkerchief and dabbed the beads of weakness from his forehead and the back of his neck.

And Jordan forgave himself.

16

CRAIG STEPPED into the staff break room after four hours on the job. He'd packed two nosebleeds—one from a pre-dawn drunken brawl and the other for a patient with hemophilia who'd tripped over her son's Lego creation and face-planted into a door jam. An emergency quick-set of three broken bones, two cardiac failure resuscitations, and removing three peanuts from a toddler's ear canal rounded out the first three of those hours. He made a mental note to check on the cardiac folks in ICU after his shift ended. Emma's spirit permeated every nook and cranny of that place, so he was glad for the ruckus with the patients. It kept his mind on task.

He would have been home on time to see how Toby fared on his first full day at Wagz without Craig. But in hour four, Eli McTilde happened, crashing his hopes for a smooth first day.

Craig checked his cell. No messages from Rhett. Or from Brian saying Rhett burned the place down. If yesterday were any indication, Toby would be doing quite well. When Craig had returned to Wagz after running

98

errands, the dog was at Rhett's side, supervising the wash-and-dry of Mr. Clayborne's cocker spaniel. Rhett was enthusiastic about having the full run of Wagz and offered to bring Toby home with him should any of Craig's shifts ever run over—as they often did in the world of emergency medicine.

Or in a world where Eli asserted himself where he wasn't needed—Like in trauma bay two where Craig had things under control.

The patient was an emotionally disturbed elderly male who'd started his morning off running through his residential neighborhood—the kind with the HOA fees—buck naked, worried the snow would hinder him from picking meatballs off his well-pruned fruit trees.

"He's been doing this all day. Fell down the stairs. Stumbled into the stove while I was boiling pasta. That's why the burn." The lady in attendance was sobbing out what had led up to the frantic 911 call and subsequent ambulance ride. The paramedics had told Craig the man was hallucinating and oblivious to pain.

Meatballs in fruit trees seems a much more benign hallucination than, say, helicopters with snipers dangling from the rails...

There was a nasty bruise on the man's hip and a neon red stripe running from his elbow to his hand. The story the lady told matched the man's injuries, and for that, Craig was glad. Too many times, he'd had to report family members for elder abuse.

On examination, the man indeed seemed oblivious to his blistering wound and the injured hip. He was mumbling about orchards and reaching for not-there meatballs when McTilde came around the corner into the curtained-off exam room after tending to a collarbone fracture from a snow-induced MVA.

"Got marinara to go with those balls?" He rolled his eyes at Craig and made the sign that the patient was intoxicated. The daughter's face flushed, and Craig turned to face his superior, standing a good head taller than McTilde. "Out."

"I'm sayin' a little parmesan and some garlic sticks would be nice, right, Mr..." Eli glanced at the computer screen displaying the patient's information, but Craig blocked his view.

"Out," Craig said again.

Eli stepped outside the curtain and nodded for Craig to join him. "Careful, Dr. Thompson. This is *my* ER, and I'll go where I please." McTilde's voice was low and raspy. Craig hoped the daughter and dad couldn't hear him.

"That's *my* patient, and you'll treat him and his family with respect." Craig made sure to speak up so there was no doubt the family—and the medical assistant in the bay with them—knew Craig meant to advocate for the distraught daughter and her dad. For added effect, Craig took a step toward him. Eli took a step backward, eyes widening, further into the hub, with staff and patients witnessing the confrontation.

Eli straightened his white coat and toyed with the end of his stethoscope, cocking his head to one side before looking Craig square in the face. "I'm sensing, Dr. Thompson, that you and I need to sit down with Mr. Underwood. And on your first day!"

"Perhaps that would be best."

"End of shift." Eli turned on his heel and disappeared into bay two to check on his own patient—where he should've been the whole time. Not harassing an elderly guy having a bad day.

Craig shook off the rising frustration of that Fourth Hour Encounter and finished a bottle of water, two bananas, and a protein bar from the community glass bowl on the breakroom table. He washed his face and made a note in his phone to bring extra sets of scrubs for his locker so he could swap for fresh ones when things get hairy.

Craig looked up from his screen to find Eli standing in his return path to the bays.

Things were sure to get hairy.

17

Melody trudged through the morning, reminding herself that the anxiety she was awash in was due to this self-inflicted project. The worry she had for Craig over his first day back tipped the needle way past concern to full-on panic. Twice since Craig left the office with his shiny new badge, she had to leave the hustle of the Courtyard and step through the exit doors down the hall. The snow was coming in bigger and bigger bursts, but the chilly winds served to dry some of her sweat.

To cover her frequent trips away from the Courtyard to stand outside, she told her co-workers she must be hitting early menopause. Mel thought at least Linda believed her and nodded her head with a genuine sympathetic bob. Old age sucks, and Linda was an expert.

Craig was only going back to Blane to help Mel sort things out. Well, not really. Craig was there solely to discover whether Emma died in vain (she did) and how to find the proof they needed to present to a legal team. The first three times Mel went, the attorney said not enough. *Circumstantial. The case was already dismissed once; you need more. A smoking gun.* And that was hard to come by when the company partially culpable for so many gun deaths never pulled a single trigger.

Mel hadn't pulled any triggers, either, but her role in the awards banquet made her feel like she had gunpowder residue all over her hands. Every. Single. Day.

Dr. T. said not so. He'd said in their quick telehealth session the other day that it might help her gain some confidence if she'd participate in the next employee appreciation event—source the hardware, the bananas, the tablecloths. He didn't care so long as she remained active and engaged.

She and he both knew what would happen to her psyche if she withdrew and started the self-blame and doubt games again.

She'd texted him about her plan with the badges. "Bold, very bold," he'd written back.

When she returned to her office, a line had begun to form with a dozen Blane Park personnel waiting to hand in their old badges and re-up with brand new ones.

Buckets and buckets of badges, and it was barely after lunch. Jordan Proctor himself oversaw the process, saying how much more efficient the new system would be to onboard new employees and upgrade or downgrade security credentials. "Proctor spared no expense in developing the tech for this upgrade. And it flows seamlessly with the upgraded protection software. Seamlessly!" Mel would nod and continue snapping employee photos, asking each one to hand over their old badge.

A couple of folks had come to work without their IDs. "That won't happen again. No badge, no clocking in. No staff is to be on the premises without ID." Mel wondered how that hard-and-fast policy would affect patient care if an on-call surgeon got called in at two a.m. to cover an emergency appendectomy and in his haste showed up without ID, but she kept her mouth shut.

Jordan went on, smiling. "We'll always know who's in the building. In any Blane Park property." Mel smiled at him and asked Carol to take over her spot at the camera so she could duck into her office away from the leering Proctor, but he tagged along after Mel instead of lording over the photos.

She sighed and waved an arm to the chair opposite her desk. "Is there something I can help you with, Mr. Proctor?" She busied herself with Craig's file. Mel was able to use Craig's photo from the morning and transfer it to the new system. She sent the file to the badge machine with a simple click of a button.

Jordan remained standing and gazed over her diploma and certifications hanging in black frames on her wall. "You worked hard to get here, yes? Are you fulfilled?"

"Sure. Blane Park is a great place to work." *Or it had been*, she refrained from tacking on.

She could hear the buzz of the badge machine down the hall. Craig's would spit out soon, and she wanted to get to it before Linda or Carol.

"Have you ever thought of quitting?"

The question caught her off guard. "Sir?"

"I mean. I imagine one can only go so far with those." He nodded toward the wall of her accomplishments. "Before one becomes...disgruntled."

She sat back in her seat, Craig's photo stared at her from the screen. Jordan's real-life mug glared a hole through her from opposite the desk. All she could do was stare back at the man blankly.

"You don't have to answer. It's just something to think

about." He glanced up at the half-circle camera in the ceiling and left her office.

She inhaled sharply, aware that she'd barely breathed since the moment he crossed the threshold of her office.

Two badges.

How did she believe she could ever pull off stealing a badge? Cameras. Linda and the higher-ups everywhere.

She stood and straightened her slacks, more to wipe the newly formed sweat from her palms, and headed around the corner to the badge machine. Forget Carol and Linda. Jordan himself beat her to it. He picked up Craig's hot-off-the-press badge and turned it over in his hand. "How's the wonder boy doing today? I'm sure you've heard something by now."

If he doesn't leave the office soon, or worse, if he tags along to the ER, she'd have to ditch the plan to keep Craig's original badge.

Think. Think.

"No, sir. I haven't heard. I was about to take that to him, so he didn't have to leave his patients unattended."

Jordan nodded and handed her the badge, leaving his grip on the edge of the photo a little too long. Then he pulled it back and stuck it in his breast coat pocket.

"Better to keep at it here. You've quite the line forming. Phone over to the bays. Tell him the CEO of Proctor Alliance would love to hand-deliver the badge personally."

Every square inch of skin on Mel's body prickled in disgust and she hoped her cheeks weren't blazing red. "Sure thing, Mr. Proctor." She swallowed hard and added, "Thank you for handling that for me. It will save a load of time."

Jordan slunk out of the Courtyard and turned left toward

the ER. She returned to her office, not daring to look overhead at the cameras. Her hand shook as she held the receiver to her ear and dialed the emergency room desk from her office phone. "Yeah. Mr. Proctor is coming with Dr. Thompson's updated badge. Just a heads-up. Thanks!" and slammed the phone down before she was forced to make small talk.

Her phone vibrated in her pocket.

Dr. T.: *How's it going? I know you're having a busy day.*

Jordan wrapped his wool coat around his waist, wishing for all he was worth for an Indian summer where the snow would abate and the temps would increase. The ambulance bay's concrete enclosure warded off the wind and snow but did little about the warmth. He'd bopped in and out of the Courtyard, watching the ladies there trying to keep up with the influx of new badge requests and turn-ins. Linda was the only one he'd trust to run that ship. The others, Melody included, weren't worth the paper their credentials were printed on.

Jordan had little trust in anyone much younger than himself, anyway, but that was beside the point.

The highlight of his morning came when he'd crept into the back corner of the ER to watch the swarm of personnel care for a patient surge. McTilde had "permitted" him to see how well the ER was running with the upgraded software and to discuss with him potentially sourcing new beds and wheelchairs. At least, that was the pretense.

The real reason for his hovering was to witness Dr. Craig Thompson in action on his first day back. The kicker came when Craig, true to form, handed off a middle-aged housewife with a nosebleed to treat a little boy in the throes of anaphylactic shock. Rage welled. Nosebleed Gal probably wouldn't smell again and be anemic the rest of her life, given that the intern treating her likely had much less skill than Craig at packing a bleed.

But Craig was all about the rush. And a boy not breathing was much more interesting than a trickle of red goo coming from someone's nose.

In his adult brain, Jordan understood this. The whole triage thing. The part of him his mother nurtured comprehended putting others first.

But the space his leg used to take up begged to differ.

As did the patients who were pushed off to the waiting rooms or left in a curtained-off hole to wonder when someone would tend to them. Jordan had been unconscious when the unthinkable happened to him.

Jordan saw lawsuits waiting to happen.

He'd addressed triage protocols with McTilde and Underwood and the managers of every hospital he'd placed in the Proctor Alliance Family of Caregivers. And they all said the same thing: That's the way medicine worked.

Some patients wait because they're in the wrong place —a walk-in clinic or an appointment with their doctors would do the trick—they didn't have to visit a trauma center for, say, a nosebleed.

But this wasn't the case for Jordan. And unless he disclosed his whole story, he would never get the answer he was searching for. He longed for someone to flat-out validate his experience: Dr. Craig Thompson neglected Jordan's care to treat a child, resulting in Jordan being less than a man.

And here it was again. Playing out in front of his eyes.

Craig pushed an adult aside and takes care of a child.

And it's only ten in the morning. He wondered how many more patients were triaged out of the way so Wonder Boy could thrive on the adrenaline that had cost Jordan his leg.

Jordan had slid Dr. Thompson's shiny new badge across the nurse's desk and gave the CNA manning the computers a wink. "Be sure he gets this." The young girl blushed and took the badge. "And shred his current one, if you wouldn't mind." She nodded.

Dr. Eli McTilde met Jordan in the darkest corner of the ambulance bay, the concrete tunnel quiet for the first time for the whole day shift. The snow squalls were relentless, wafting in and out of the bay, flapping Jordan's suit lapels open, forcing him to button it, and sending visible drafts up Dr. McTilde's white coat, puffing him up in the chest more than he already was. Jordan recalled the slide-off he'd seen earlier today, and ERs across Indianapolis had likely treated dozens of patients thanks to the quick glaze of slick over the roadways.

With the Midwest weather tantrums, tomorrow, the ERs could be full of heat strokes.

Eli was yammering on about some meatball man and how Craig had humiliated him in front of the staff. "You'd better cool your jets. At least for a while. Don't let your ego get in the way of our objective."

"I'm not sure our objectives are the same, Jordan. Underwood's gunning for me. I know it."

Jordan cringed. He disliked being on a first-name basis with Eli, but necessity and all... "Underwood's an idiot. He'll do or say anything I ask him to save a buck and keep Blane out of the red."

"He's a coward, but he's not stupid." Eli turned a shoulder toward the wind.

Jordan disagreed. In the years of working with the CEO of Blane, Jordan found Underwood trusted but never verified and, much like McTilde, was more impressed by putting on a show than ensuring the quality of staff and equipment. The holographic logo floating above Indianapolis was a case in point. Did Eli have any idea how much Underwood spent on such trivial branding? "When are you meeting with Craig again?"

"I demanded a sit-down with Underwood at the end of shift this evening. Discuss the hierarchy of the trauma bays and, well, test how far Craig's ego runs."

"Not as deeply as yours does, Dr. McTilde." Jordan ignored the cringe from his cohort and thought while he massaged his thigh with a gloved hand. He wasn't sure Eli was thinking straight, but he'd better throw the guy a bone lest he blow up the scaffolding. "Perhaps a leave of absence right out of the gate would do Craig good, if you really need to show him whose boss. He's not top dog here. Keep him off his game, but stay on yours."

"A leave? I get what we're doing, but we are truly short-staffed in the bays—"

"Which you have been for months. You can't have it both ways. Craig takes leave or you stay quiet. If he goes, you can survive a few more days."

Doubt raced across Eli's face. Jordan could see why the man was always in Craig Thompson's shadow. Always second-guessing himself. Always whining. "Man up. Put him on leave the rest of the week for insubordination." Jordan reached for his stump before he could stop himself, rubbing the place where the silicone sleeve contacted the skin.

"Still giving you trouble?" Eli asked.

"You're no Craig Thompson. So yes, Eli. It still gives me trouble."

Eli cringed. Perhaps Jordan hadn't forgiven him after all. He waved Eli back toward the ER. "Underwood will go for it if you're forceful enough." Jordan smiled for the first time in three days. "And then we'll really rock Thompson's boat."

"What will you be doing in the meantime?"

Jordan pulled his coat tighter around him. "I have a plane to catch. Blane isn't my only enterprise, you know."

19

THE MEETING in Underwood's office started promptly at the end of Craig's first shift. More than once through the rest of the day, a smirking McTilde pointed his lanky finger to the ceiling, indicating the fourth-floor CEO's suite.

He shuffled in the waiting area, and for the first time, inspected his upgraded badge. Mel was able to use the same pic, so that saved him another encounter with her in HR. He couldn't see much difference between this and the other as he turned the card over in his hand. His name in bold and all caps. Blane Park in all caps alternating with the Caring Hands logo repeated in the background. Security stripe on the back. A silver chip, smaller than the ones on his credit cards, next to the stripe—

Alfred's secretary finally waved him into the C-suite when it was clear Craig would rather pace than take a seat. Opulent was an understatement. Glass from floor to ceiling framed the Indy skyline. Craig preferred the view from Crown Hill, slightly hazy and much more peaceful. At night, Alfred could certainly sit here and admire the Caring

Hands holograph in all its glory spin above Salesforce Tower.

Framed photos lined the mahogany desk—one held Craig's attention. McTilde, Underwood, and a man Craig didn't recognize leaning against a jet-black Ferrari, Underwood dangling the keys above his head with a goofy grin on his face...

Craig hadn't fully processed the whole of the office before Underwood spoke, his baritone voice bouncing off the rich wood and marble surfaces.

"Well, this isn't exactly how I saw our first sit-down going, Craig. I asked you to keep an eye on him, not flip his crazy switch."

Craig pulled away from the photo and took a breath. "Nice ride." Then, "Eli is a disaster of a human and has no regard for patients. But you already know that, right? Isn't that what you wanted confirmation of?"

"I know the chip on his shoulder sprouted a dozen more when he heard you were coming back." Nodding toward the frame, "It is an exceptional vehicle."

"Eli's chips are—" Craig stopped himself before saying too much too soon. "Patient care should come first, no matter what I think of the man personally. *He* offended my patient and family, left *his* patient alone before the assessment was done—"

Eli strode into the office and flopped into the seat next to Craig. He reached over to the desk and straightened the Ferrari's frame. Craig wondered how long he'd lingered in the doorway. Eli's coat was still crisp and white. Craig became acutely aware of the state of his own scrubs after the long day. But, you can keep a white coat clean when you stay arm's length from your duties.

"You get my email, Al?"

Underwood glared at Eli over his glasses and clicked the mouse. "Mr. Underwood, in this setting, Dr. McTilde." More mouse clicking. "Yes. I got the email. It appears you *gentlemen* need to learn how to coexist in the bays."

Eli kept on. "You can see there, due to his insubordination right out of the gate, and seeing as how Dr. Thompson is well aware of Blane's standard of conduct since having been employed here previously, I have recommended suspension."

Alfred laughed and leaned back in his chair with his fingers interlocked behind his head. "You're short-handed, Dr. McTilde. Very much so. I've tasked you with recruiting, which you've done, but no one stays. Why is that? And now Dr. Thompson has walked in off the streets with a skill set most metropolises would kill for, and you want him out on day one?" Alfred cocked his head slightly and looked at Craig. "Play nice, boys."

Eli tried again. "I wonder about his stability—"

Craig seethed but said nothing. *Inhale, exhale.*

"Eli, we're done here."

Eli raised a hand to add to the conversation, but Alfred brought his palms down to the mahogany with a smack. "We are *done*."

All three men rose. The doctors left the C-suite, leaving a red-faced Mr. Underwood to brood in silence.

Craig intended to take the stairs down to the main level since Eli was heading toward the elevator. Neither man made it to their respective targets before the Crash Code sounded. All available medical staff to Emergency.

In two strides, Craig was through the fourth-floor stairwell, and McTilde was right behind. With each turn in the stairwell, the doctors' footsteps echoed. Adrenaline rushing, Craig couldn't help but increase his speed and hope that he could manage to put an entire floor between himself and Eli.

He did with ease. Eli was out of breath before hitting the first-floor landing.

The trauma bays were hopping. A massive crash from I-465 had brought multiple victims. Craig resisted the impulse to coordinate—that was Eli's job. Dr. McTilde visibly inhaled, took a second to survey the patient load, smiled, and sent Craig to bay two.

Without hesitation, Craig entered the bay and assessed his patient. A 15-year-old who'd been a backseat passenger in a car that had flipped over the concrete meridian. Multiple contusions and a protruding bone from the left forearm. Craig ordered internal scans and a full panel of X-rays to assess for internal damage.

His team whisked the boy away to the imaging suite, and Craig used the moments to make notes in the boy's electronic chart on the massive touchscreen monitor hanging from the wall. He was about to step out and see where else to be of use when Eli popped his head through the curtain. "Don't let him lose any limbs, Wonder Boy."

Craig focused on his patient's monitor, tapping impatiently on the table beneath it, hoping the digital imaging would upload quickly and Craig could focus on proceeding with his patient instead of wondering how Eli had the time to snark when the bays were full.

Eli didn't move. "I bet this brings back painful memories, yes? How to keep your patient from dying in the same bay where poor Emma was shot?"

Craig whipped his head around. "What did you say to

me?" The monitor above him dinged several times, indicating the digital X-rays had hit the system for review.

Eli stood firm. Smug. Nodded to the monitor and pointed not at it, but behind it. Craig followed his aim. There, mostly masked by the large screen, was a photo of his Emma shellacked to a plaque. The text beneath danced in his vision as his mind spun, he couldn't get the words to stay still long enough to read them.

"Your *girlfriend* did that. Well, between the time she was your girlfriend and then mine. And then yours again."

Black specks dotted his periphery. Then sheets of red closed in.

In a smooth motion, Craig made one stride, rose his right fist, and made contact with Eli's nose, sending the pompous doctor skidding on his ass out of the bay and across the freshly buffed ER floor.

Smack in the middle of the mass Code, the emergency room went still. Witnesses stood in stunned silence as Eli remained on the floor, holding his nose, blood seeping through his fingers. Huge tears poured from Eli's eyes, mixing with the red.

Craig turned back to the plaque. *In Memory of a True Hero.* That's as far as he got before slumping against the wall, rubbing his knuckles.

He didn't know how long he sat there—seconds, a minute? Underwood had appeared behind the bloody Eli. Nurses started to move back to their patients and a couple toward Eli. Trevor rounded the corner with his cart, taking in the scene. He wheeled over to Craig, a proud smirk starting, and helped him to his feet. "Hooyah, Doc," Trevor whispered in his ear as he stood with a hand on Craig's chest.

Alfred glared into bay two, his baritone voice bellowed through the whole department. "*Now* you're suspended."

And Eli grinned.

Grinned through the blood and the snot and tears pouring from his face.

Craig's rage flared. He balled his fists again, and leaned hard into Trevor's steady hand, but the old guy was solid. "Easy there, bud. Just let it fall. Not worth it."

Craig focused on his friend's face and breathed. Trevor was right.

At the very least, that jackass's coat wasn't white anymore.

20

"It was a nice gesture." Craig toyed with the tablecloth the same way Mel had that first day she waited for him at The Sicilian. The caddy and that stupid candle worked their way to the middle of the table. She gently pushed it all back. Craig put his hands back in his lap.

Mel told herself she wasn't going to cry. She did what she did. She'd remembered the memorial in plenty of time to do something about it, then had forgotten almost as quickly. "I'm so sorry, Craig. I never imagined you'd ever—"

"Ever see it or ever work at Blane again?"

"Either."

They both shifted in the booth. The waitress, Sadie from that very first time, came for their orders—a small pizza to share and salads—and the silence hung for a long, tense moment.

"He did it on purpose, Mel. Eli didn't triage that MVA mess based on any physician skill or patient need. He'd have sent me to bay two if it held an 80-year-old with hemorrhoids. He did it on purpose and baited me to find it." Craig rubbed the knuckles of his right hand.

Mel winced. "I'm so, so sorry. I was going to ask Trevor to take it down—"

"It's not about the memorial, don't you get it? Eli wanted me on suspension from the get-go. Alfred said as much in our meeting. He used Emma to get it done."

Another long pause.

"He used *you*, too, Mel."

She fought the urge to excuse herself to the restroom where she could fire off a panicked text to Dr. T. He could send her one of his quick one-liners, a lifeline out of this turmoil...

"It must've ended really badly between you and Eli, yes?" Craig's tone softened a bit. He must've sensed her agony.

She swallowed hard. *Come clean.* "He didn't strike me as caring one bit. We only had a few dates. Not enough for something like this."

"Clearly, you struck a nerve with him."

"I think it's more about his bruised ego in your shadow. Ever since high school..."

"This can't just be about a high school grudge. No way. Not even Eli."

Sadie came with their salads. "Pizza'll be a few more minutes."

"Underwood wanted me to keep an eye on him, report in." Craig fiddled with the dressing packet.

Mel was about to stab a tomato but paused, fork midair. "What?"

"Alfred wanted me to give him a direct report on Eli's performance in the ER. Caught me in the hallway and tasked me with it this morning." Craig dropped his fork, not taking a bite, and rubbed his hands through his hair. "What a day."

As if on cue, the entry door chimed, and Eli waltzed into The Sicilian. Mel saw him coming. Craig had not, his head in his hands now and staring at the table. She tried to nudge him under the table, to get him to pay attention, lest he come up out of his pause in a continued rant. Her foot connected with his shin as Eli reached their booth.

"Well, well, well. Imagine seeing you here." Eli grinned at Mel, then turned toward Craig. "And with the grand and glorious Dr. Thompson himself. I'd be careful hanging out with this one, though. He's a bit of a rebel these days." Back to Mel, and in a sneer, "Wouldn't want his bad habits rubbing off on you. Would be something to discuss with Dr. T., yes?"

Until that moment, she knew she'd been flushed and red-faced with embarrassment trying to explain herself to Craig. At Eli's appearance, the blood pooled in her core, and she longed to bolt. Eli was blocking her exit, and then the pizza came.

"Oh, y'all need another place?" Sadie balanced the pizza pan above her shoulder and turned to Eli. "Oh... oh. Maybe I should bring an ice pack, too?"

It was Eli's turn to turn red. He stepped back and ducked his head.

"He's already had the opportunity for medical treatment." Craig patted a place on the table for the pizza. "We won't need an extra place setting. He's leaving."

Mel kept her head down and did not engage. She sensed Eli stepping away. "We're not done yet, Dr. Thompson."

Sadie had to step around Eli, and before she could get the pan to the table, Craig said, "We'll need a couple of boxes, please."

The door chimed again as Eli left. Mel could barely

raise her head to meet Craig's gaze. "Dr. T.? What is going on, Mel? He isn't making any sense." Craig's irritation had turned to hurt. She saw it in his face. The same look he had when he talked about Emma.

Mel honestly had no idea. This was over the top, even for someone as jealous as Eli. She regretted ever having gotten involved with him. Regretted telling him about her therapy appoint—

Her mind spun and she couldn't keep her thoughts in order.

"I never told him that." Chills across her chest. Hands trembling.

"Told him what?" Craig's irritation was growing.

"I mean. I told him I was seeing someone, but I never said who. I know I didn't. I never told him who I was seeing."

Sadie showed up with the check and the boxes for their pizza. "You guys never eat when you're here, you know that?"

Mel rolled her eyes and began shoving pizza slices into both boxes, burning her fingers. "That creep. He went snooping. He must've gotten into my files at Blane and found out about my therapy appointments."

She fought back white-hot tears. What had been nagging at the back of her mind was bubbling up to the surface. She pushed her salad plate away and covered her face with her hands.

From bubbles to a full wave. The realization that *he's* talking. Dr. T's talking. Broken the sacred veil of confidentiality. To what end? And how long ago?

Remain active and engaged.

Asking specifics about her plans.

Source the bananas or tablecloths.

"Oh, god." She was going to be sick. "They're setting me up. Or they want me to quit. Or. I don't know. But they're both in on it."

"Mel?" Craig tried to reach for her, but she pulled back and could barely look at him. "We aren't seeing each other. Did you tell him that we are?"

"What? No. Not you. Oh god... Another Dr. T. Nooo... Not that way. Therapy. Counseling." She let out a moan. It was all too much.

"What are you talking about? Melody, what does Eli have on you?" Craig's eyes widened and she stifled a sob. "What have you told him?" Craig paused with the rapid-fire questions. She watched confusion spread across his face. "He's the reason. *You're* the reason this is coming undone?" She'd not blame him if he never spoke to her again.

Déjà vu played out in slow motion. Craig rose, left a wad of cash—enough to cover the meal and tip Sadie—and left.

He left her alone, with two boxes of untouched pizza, a mess of her own making, and an unlit candle.

21

Jordan bellied up to the least crowded bar, carefully maneuvering his leg so passerby travelers couldn't tell he wasn't a whole man. He looked around his shoulder, seeing if anyone was staring or pointing as his metal shin clanked against the elevated stool. He preferred drinking in the comfort of one of his penthouses and felt all eyes on him in this pitiful "island oasis" at Indy International.

"Bourbon, two cubes."

Deep breath in, long exhale out.

He knew his blood pressure was elevated after the security issue and hadn't returned to baseline yet. As usual, his bullet-proof documentation for his prosthetic leg hadn't been enough. The screening monster in the TSA uniform pulled him aside and frisked his entire being—not just his leg. Small miracle he managed to keep his mouth shut and put up with the disgrace.

Jordan sat back on the stool, watching the travelers. A bedraggled set of parents pulled two sleepy children behind them; the girl drug her blanket on the ground. A stuffed puppy wiggled from the little boy's backpack and fell near

Jordan's stool. No one saw. Jordan didn't bother to alert them. The world doesn't play fair. The child may as well learn that lesson early.

He rubbed his stump. It could've been worse—once he'd been tossed in a room and asked to remove his prosthesis entirely. That was in Texas. But today was enough to warrant a strong drink before catching his flight to LaGuardia. Proctor Alliance's board was meeting, and he wanted to be there in person. He'd seen enough at Blane this morning to have faith that McTilde had been put in his place. Dr. T. was certainly coming through, and Jordan would return to Indiana in plenty of time before the benefit banquet. As much as he'd rather stay in Manhattan, he wasn't about to miss the show here in the Hoosierland.

The bartender put his drink in front of him. Three cubes.

Before he could take her to task, his phone buzzed, alerting him of a text. Eli. Again. Perhaps Jordan's faith was too quickly placed. He used his index finger to fish out the rogue ice cube and flicked it behind the bar.

Eli: *Saw the couple. Engaged like you said.*

Jordan: *I didn't say to engage. I said to buy us some time and get him suspended.*

Eli: *I think they're cooking something up. Got to be. But they're not dating, by the looks of it.*

Jordan let out a moan. The bartender turned toward him, but he waved her incompetent skillset back to whatever she was busy doing. He was about to wave off Eli's behavior as a minor slight, but after the incident and the doctor's wounded ego...

Jordan: *What did you say, exactly?*

He sipped his drink as he watched the typing dots come and go and come again. Jordan would be in his limo in NYC before Eli could text out a simple message.

Then the phone rang, as he knew it would.

He answered and listened quietly to Eli's retelling of the events at the restaurant. Jordan stood and stretched. No chance his blood pressure would return to normal anytime this week. He picked up the toy the boy had lost.

A tiny, dirty little mutt, indeed.

On the phone one more time, he turned the toy over in his hands. "I need you back at the airport ASAP. And I'll need your daughter's dog for a day." Nate may be the only truly competent man on his team now. With a smirk, he tossed the stuffed animal to the floor and downed the rest of his drink.

Then Jordan hurled the bourbon glass at the mirrored wall above the bar, glass shattering in all directions.

He smoothed his suit. "I said two cubes."

22

CRAIG MANAGED TO SHAVE—SOMETHING he didn't have time to do before his first shift—bypassed the stack of scrubs laid out for what would've been wardrobe choices for the rest of the week, and went for jeans and a ratty T-shirt. He'd spent last night on the couch, effectively putting himself to bed with no supper after what was the second-longest day of his life, the first being the day Emma died. The stress of the first day back. The reason he went back in the first place. Alfred. Eli. Bloody noses. Suspension.

And that look on Mel's face all over again at The Sicilian...

After dropping the third tennis ball on Craig's chest with no luck at enticing him into a game, Toby had fussed on the floor next to the couch all night, no doubt wondering why they weren't in the bedroom curled up under the blankets. What little sleep Craig did get was interrupted by the dog's rustling. Yet, neither of them bothered to move from their places of misery.

Craig stared at the ceiling most of the night, bemoaning ever getting involved with Mel in any way—back in high school or present-day disasters. He should've kept his nose in his own lane, kept the keys to Wagz in his own pocket, and never given Blane or the shootings anything more than a passing thought.

His stomach was still in a knot, so he skipped breakfast, brushed his teeth, and called for Toby to leash him. That knot served to remind him he'd been rude to Mel—again. He knew it. That wasn't in his nature, and he cringed at the thought, but wow. The secrets she's kept. The position she put him in...

The streets were clear. Monday's snow squalls and dark clouds all melted away, replaced with bright blue sky and warm enough that he went back in to change his coat for a lighter jacket. Too bad Mother Nature couldn't change up yesterday's events like it changed up the weather. At least the ERs won't have to worry about snow-related accidents today. Today it'll be falls from ladders, heart attacks, and strokes.

Like that's your problem now. You fell for Eli's bait and now you get to watch dogs take baths...

Craig tried to shake off the self-hate and focused on the drive to Wagz, where he and Toby jumped out of the Jeep as Brian was struggling to open Rivers Realty's back door with a stack of files in one arm and Hackett's lead wound around his opposite wrist. Leashing Hackett became a must due to the dog's newfound interest in Clarence. HearClearly's audiologist and dog-lover at heart had started bringing treats for Hackett, Toby, and all of Wagz's clients. Both Rhett and Brian had tried to get Clarence to stop, but the expectation was already etched in Hackett's brain.

Craig was about to give Brian a hand when Clarence arrived and parked next to Craig's Jeep. Toby started to sneak off for his treat until Craig yelled, "Heel," then the lab stopped and returned to Craig.

Hackett had other ideas, and in one swift motion, he lunged toward HearClearly. Brian couldn't get unwound from the human end of the lead, Craig was useless at the angle he stood, and Hackett was off. In cartoon fashion, Brian's folders flew in all directions and the man fairly flopped around at the end of the leash, arm fully extended, barely able to stay on his feet and completely failing to halt the retired police pooch.

After securing Toby inside Wagz, Craig ran to help. Clarence was apologizing profusely, having dropped the box he'd been carrying, sending state-of-the-art blue-tooth hearing aids all over the back lot. Hackett was trampling over all of them, searching for a doggie biscuit. "If there's anything I can ever do, please let me know. I had no idea I'd cause this much trouble." Brian was apologizing through gritted teeth to Clarence for the more-than-likely ruined products.

Craig diagnosed Brian's injury by the wince and the way he cradled that arm. He unwound the lead from Brian's wrist and helped him to his feet, careful not to touch that left side. "I think Hackett dislocated your shoulder."

"Gee. Doc. I'd have never guessed."

Brian's uncharacteristic grump sealed the diagnosis.

"You can give him a lift in doc, right? You headed that way?" Clarence busied himself picking up the hearing aids.

"Well..." Craig was hesitant to explain why he wasn't heading to the ER this morning. Hackett still pulled on the lead, eager to search through more of the fallen packages. "Hackett, Heel!" The dog's head snapped back and he sat on his haunches, looking up at Craig with shock.

"Traitor," Brian mumbled under his breath. Then,

"Can't you just, um..." Brian aimed his shoulder toward Craig.

"Here?" Of course, Craig could, but an X-ray and controlled environment would be best.

"I'm country tough and don't much like hospitals."

Craig didn't much like hospitals anymore, either. "Still..."

"Trauma doc, right? If I promise not to sue?"

Clarence stepped up, having cleaned up the hearing aid carnage. "I can hold him down for you. Least I could do."

Good grief. Craig tied the end of Hackett's lead to the front fender of Clarence's sedan. "Come here." He told Clarence to stand behind Brian—more to catch him if he were to faint than to be Craig's impromptu support staff.

Craig started by feeling around the humerus to confirm the bone had indeed popped out of socket. It had. Hackett did a thorough job. "You're gonna want to follow up with your own doc. And an X-ray." Before Craig got out "ray," he'd popped Brian's shoulder back into its socket. Clarence proved his value by easing Brian down to the pavement as the realtor moaned in agony. "And pain meds. You could do with some pain meds."

Clarence stood back, arms crossed over his chest, looking down at Brian. "Or a good hooker and some cocaine would be another option." He pointed to Brian's left arm. "But I guess that depends on how much work the hooker wants to do."

Craig and Brian's eyes widened in unison. "I, uh..." Brian's face reddened, and Craig once again helped the stammering man regain his footing.

"Seriously, man. If there's ever anything. I shoulda listened to you guys weeks ago when you told me to stop bringing the treats. I wanted to be a good neighbor. Love dogs, too."

"It's all good, Clarence." Brian waved him off as Clarence unwound the leash from his bumper and handed it back to Craig.

"Hey. While you're both out here. And bad timing, I know. But is your rent going up?"

Craig thought it was an odd question and that Clarence was referring to the rent on his bungalow.

"It's happening all over Bella Square. At least all those spots owned by the same corporation." Brian said, eeking out the words, but seemed glad to focus on something other than what had to be terrible pain.

"Wait. Our *business* rent went up?" Craig felt about as bright as Toby. After establishing Wagz, he'd set everything to come out from the business account automatically. He'd probably seen a notice, and in the whirlwind of ever-present grief and Blane Park folders, it didn't register.

"Several days ago," Clarence said.

"The rent increase already hit several properties around here, the one across the street and over on Parades Parkway that I know of—there are probably more." Brian babied his arm, hugging it to his chest.

"I've been so engrossed in starting back at the ER I hadn't noticed it yet."

"We should buy out. Save a ton of money in the long run. And we could control who goes into that empty space." Brian, ever the businessman.

Craig's head spun. "I'll have to look into it."

Clarence shifted the box of hearing aids on his hip. "Seriously. If you ever need anything. Give me the go-ahead and I'll hack the owner. Dig up some dirt. Negotiation ammunition." Clarence practically glowed.

Brian and Craig stared at Clarence again. "I'm kidding about the hooker. And the coke. Well, kinda. I'm not kidding about the hacking. This job," He jutted his face toward HearClearly, "at least lets me tinker with electronics without violating my parole." He grinned. Brian and Craig continued to stare. "Blink, guys. I'm not gonna hack *you*."

The men laughed it off. Craig led a disappointed Hackett to Rivers Realty and reminded Brian to have a follow-up with his doctor as soon as possible. He made a mental note to upgrade the firewall protection and change his passwords.

Clarence. Who knew?

Toby was whining from inside the back door. Rhett had already started on the day's clients. "I figured you had your hands full outside." He couldn't stifle a grin, and Craig allowed himself a quick laugh about it out of sight and earshot of Brian.

"It was quite the show for a few minutes."

Winston was in the bath again so soon. This time it was flour and play-dough. Craig wasn't sure what Diane was doing in that prissy home of hers that this dog kept getting into messes.

Craig went to his office, where Rhett had dutifully stacked the business mail on the filing cabinet, unopened. Craig flipped through and found the letter his business neighbors had alluded to. The return address section made his palms sweat. The same name was on multiple documents Mel had unearthed.

The company that owned the ground under Wagz was a subsidiary of none other than Proctor Alliance.

23

CRAIG CAME out of the office, stuffing the rent letter in his back pocket. Toby rose from Rhett's side and greeted him.

"Would you mind hanging on to Toby for a while? I've got some, well…"

"Yeah, Doc. No problem. Hey, I thought you'd be on shift all day anyway."

"About that…" Craig summed up the previous day's issues and then assured Rhett he wasn't going to lay him off from Wagz. "Your job is safe. Especially with all I've got going on to clean up my reputation." Craig didn't offer more. It wasn't Rhett's place to help past running the grooming and watching over Toby.

"No problem, boss. Take as long as you need. We'll be fine."

Craig bent and loved on Tobes for a quick moment, then drove his Jeep back to the bungalow. The pages of evidence flapped in the register vent's draft. He tacked the rent letter on the wall next to Mel's email and highlighted Proctor's name. He highlighted in yellow every mention of Proctor Alliance he could find in all of the documents.

He found a lot.

He highlighted every mention of Proctor's founder, a Mr. Jordan Proctor, in blue—only found a couple of mentions. He made Alfred's name green, and that was only associated with Blane's side of things.

He stood back to examine the wall and got lost in it all. No wonder the lawyers said Mel had no case. About the time he found a thread, it unwound and... nothing.

He couldn't see how the pieces fit, but he knew they did. What was it Mel had said? That they were setting her up? A therapist and Eli? That made no sense. But she'd made no sense last night at The Sicilian, clearly distraught over the whole matter.

Why Mel?

Why random properties in Bella Square that had nothing at all to do with the medical complex?

What was that famous line in every mystery ever written? Follow the money? He wrote that down on a notecard and tacked it to the wall.

Blane Park would have money eventually—a lot of it— but despite its showy exterior, the complex was in its infancy, and any siphoning of funds would certainly be noticed.

And Mel had no money—she still Ubered everywhere, for crying out loud. There was nothing to gain from involving her.

Or was there?

C'mon, Craig, think. Where was that near-photographic memory of his when he needed it the most?

He picked up one of Toby's tennis balls. Bounced it on the floor, it careened off the evidence wall and landed back in his hand.

Again. Bounce. Careen. Catch. Over and over. The

thumping drowning out the vent, the traffic on the street, the pounding of the pulse in his ears...

What if it's not about money? He tossed the ball into the kitchen. He tore down that card and wrote a new one: "Follow the motive" and tacked it up at the very top.

On another card, he wrote "Eli wants my suspension." On another he scribbled "Alfred wants info on Eli." A third read "Therapist leaks Mel's info to Eli?"

What did Mel have that Proctor or Blane needed? Craig knew she'd overcome a lot—including their breakup and the tragedies that befell Indy during the shootings, but neither her degree nor her job gained her access to anything special behind the scenes at Blane that Craig could see.

Breathe.

What's the next move?

He read and re-read Mel's email. There was something there, he could feel it. Or something with that therapist...

The email discussed The Caring Hands Banquet... Alfred wanting things to move along fast.

Move fast. Ferraris are fast.

The photo, front and center in Underwood's office, with Alfred and Eli and that car. And that man he'd not recognized in the photo, but who he'd seen before. Just a glimpse during Craig's very first time back on Blane's campus. Limping but not limping. Dressed to impress.

Dressed to hide an imperfection.

It hit him like a wave, the memories flooding back in rapid succession.

Craig fished through his contacts for Emma's best friend — Samantha in medical records at Mount Lombard. He cringed as he threw that connection and his current credentials around to get access to yet another set of files. "It's for Emma, Sam."

A pause on the line.

"I'll send it encrypted."

"Thanks."

Craig waited on the couch with his laptop, leg bobbing up and down in anticipation, but confident he knew what he'd see in the medical records from all those years ago.

His notification dinged.

He clicked open the first two files: Dead on arrival. An Angela Proctor, MVA on the George Washington, and an Evan Forester.

The last file: Jordan Proctor. MVA George Washington Bridge. Attending: Dr. Craig Thompson, second: Dr. Eli McTilde. Amputation.

Mel was right. They're setting her up.

Eli and Tanberg.

Jordan Proctor.

But it wasn't about her...

Then he called the only man he knew that had any shot of getting him what he needed from the icy depths of Blane Park—A Navy man.

24

Mel barely made it through the workday. Linda. Carol. Riki and her endless, bubble-head emails. Budget. New Hires. Alfred on her case. Banquet plans. She went into robo-mode, one task after another. The Courtyard was buzzing with different renditions of how Dr. Thompson sent Dr. McTilde flying across the ER hub. More buzz about Craig's suspension and how long he'd be gone.

All her fault.

She finally made it home, a sweaty, miserable wreck. She changed into sweats, her baggiest hoodie, and flopped into bed, sobbing face-down into her pillow while Omega sat on her head. Demon cat, yes, but in similar butt-on-head fashion, the feline had gotten her through multiple failed first dates—including the fiasco with Eli.

Omega, along with the sessions with Dr. T.

But Tanberg had betrayed her—not only her, but that oh-so-vital oath to hold patient confidentiality in the highest regard.

She'd trusted him. Had trusted Craig. Had tried with Eli.

How much breaking can one heart handle before it won't mend again?

Dr. T. had used her, and Eli helped. And all because of something she had absolutely nothing to do with—a high school romance she'd put too much stock in, their breakup, and a reunion nightmare.

She should have seen the signs. Dr. Tanberg had been so much more interested in her every move of late. Her every thought about anything related to Blane and the shootings.

Her comings... *What are your plans this weekend? Because it's important to have a social life.*

Her goings... *What hours do you intend to work? Because it's important to establish routines.*

Ugg. How did she ever think she could outwit the entities behind defective weapons software when she missed such obvious signs in her very few personal relationships?

And what mental health pro makes enough green to own a Mercedes Coupe? The photo showed up in Tanberg's office a year ago, maybe. Him, that car, and his glee-smitten passengers waving their arms outside the vehicle. She and who knows how many others have been shelling out copays for therapy, but no amount of crazy could pay for *that* model.

She should've left well enough alone. Should've listened to Dr. T. months ago when he said to leave things be. She was paying him for his advice, after all. Should've never printed that email out.

Drove it to Wagz.

Taped it to the door.

She rose from the bed, sending Omega thudding to the floor, requesting tuna for his trouble. She wiped her eyes on her sleeves and went to the kitchen to oblige him and pull herself together. She'd love, love, love to take the day off work tomorrow and spend it crying into Omega's fur. And day-drinking.

Day drinking would numb the pain, at least at first.

She stroked Omega's fur as he slurped his gooey treat from his dish.

Her phone buzzed in her back pocket.

Craig.

Her heart sank and then flipped. In the two seconds it took her to answer, her brain concocted a dozen scenarios. *He's apologizing. He's suing me. He hates me. He's coming back to work. He's leaving the country. He loves—wait.*

Loves me? *Oh, Mel. Flip that candle upside down already.*

"Hi." *Breathe.*

"Hi. We need to talk."

"Probably. Probably." *Genius, Mel.*

"I've been mulling over all the parts of this mess, and I think I may have found the thread."

"What?" She was on high alert now, waiting for his response.

"I don't want to discuss it over the phone. Can I see you?"

"K."

"*Not* at The Sicilian."

"K." Fine with her. She didn't want to deal with Sadie and her lighter again so soon. Or risk running into anyone else from Blane Park.

She had an hour, less than, to gather herself. How would she be able to look at him? When she instigated their little covert investigation, she couldn't have foreseen the outcome. Like she couldn't have anticipated disaster or seen the outcome of choosing a venue last year. A dozen little pieces of advice and encouragement floated through her brain—all in Dr. T.'s voice. She shook her head. She didn't want his voice in there anymore.

She didn't want Craig's defeated expression floating around up there, either.

But here we go. She splashed water on her face, put on her raggedy Colts baseball cap with shaking hands, and called for her Uber.

This meet-up will stink as bad as Omega's tuna.

25

Snowflakes swirled around Mel as she bobbed up and down, rubbing her hands together for warmth. Today's earlier teaser of 50 degrees and sunny pushed thoughts of winter wear far out of her mind. As evening approached, the clouds thickened and winter knocked on the door. Those gloves on her counter would've been nice.

Crown Hill's mortuary housed her grandparents. They'd opted for a pair of burgundy urns for themselves and a tiny purple box for their prized cat. Mel's mother blew a gasket when she realized they'd prepaid for Mozart's final arrangements before they decided on their own final resting place. Mel'd not thought about what to do with Omega. Or herself. She hoped at least one of his nine lives would outlive her one and she'd not have to deal with any of it. Dr. Tan—

She caught herself and shook her head. How long will this go on?

Lots of that. Dr. Tanberg had made a nest in her head and lived there—quite loudly.

Craig's Jeep finally pulled into the spot where her Uber

had dropped her. Toby wasn't with him. What did she think? That he'd bring the dog to the mausoleum?

Before he left the vehicle, Craig nodded a greeting—one as cold as the wind. The pair made their way into the building where it was barely any warmer. They walked in silence—Mel slightly ahead of him, leading the way to her grandparents' display.

Without looking back, she offered an "I'm sorry." Her voice broke. She'd held back vital information from Craig. He never had the full picture of her and Eli, let alone Dr. Tanberg, and it'd cost them the chance to make things right for Emma and the other victims.

And she'd known it from that first night at The Sicilian. She'd been close to telling him about Eli but held back. Despite epic embarrassment over getting involved with him, she'd truly believed Eli had nothing to do with this mess. "I'm sorry," she offered again, in case he hadn't heard the first time. And because it made her feel a microscopic bit better to say it a second time.

"I know, Mel. But that's not what I'm after. Apologies, I mean." Craig's voice, even muffled, echoed off the marble walls. He winced and lowered the volume another notch. "He's a serious problem. Eli."

The bench where Mel had sat comforting her mom on more than one occasion was even more uncomfortable than it had been on the day they'd put Granddad here. She sat, not expecting Craig to join her, but he did. They stared at the wall of drawers and cubbies holding cremains. She watched as Craig's eyes scanned the names, pausing as he found her family. "The purple trinket box?"

"Mozart."

"Their cat? I bet that went over well with your mother."

"You've no idea."

Craig chuckled a little, and Mel relaxed. "What would you like me to do next? I'll do anything to make up—"

"You don't have anything to make up for. I need complete transparency. Not the—" he hesitated, rubbing his knuckles. "Not the dark details of your sessions, of course. Anything about plans you had with the information you'd gathered. Anything relating to Emma or Eli—" he hesitated again. "Or me."

It was her turn to wince. She wasn't the only one feeling awkward. Tears escaped and ran down her face. She wiped them and shifted her gaze to the huge stained-glass window. A thin, brown tree worked its way up the panes surrounded by purple flowers. Various birds sat among the branches. It was so much prettier when backlit by brilliant sunlight, every tiny detail exploding from the glass. With only the dim interior light this evening, it wasn't nearly as impressive.

Craig leaned forward, his movement breaking through her mini zone-out. He rested his elbows on his knees, head in his hands. "They'll use it against me. Against us."

She swallowed hard, thinking of the intimate details she'd spilled to Dr. T. over the years. The months of being completely frozen in depression and indecision. She stood up and approached her grandparents' little glassed-in niche. Together forever.

She'd once thought that would be her and Craig in eighty years—a forever relationship. Someone to build a life with. Good, bad, all the in-betweens. Jobs and kids and vacations...

Eternally bonded with your one true love. Something she'd divulged in her sessions. She thought Dr. T. was helping her move past this shattered imagined future to paint a new one for herself.

Her gut knotted at the betrayal, and she was glad she hadn't eaten anything since breakfast.

She remembered Eli's face from The Sicilian, swollen and bruised and smirking. How he'd baited Craig. How he'd used her. How they both had used her. Steam rose from within, and she no longer felt the cold.

"Mel?" Craig prompted.

She ran a hand over the glass separating her from the burgundy urns, then turned to the window again.

It was time to shed light on the whole thing. From every angle possible.

Light it up.

"I'll tell you everything."

26

CRAIG LISTENED as Mel spilled out her last few years' worth of secrets. Tears fell down her cheeks and her words bounced off the marble walls of the mausoleum. Sometimes her voice echoed down the hallway, and he feared someone would hear, but he didn't interrupt her. She was opening up, and he needed to hear. He got the feeling she needed this, too.

He knew there were darker days she didn't reveal to him. She didn't need to go there, and he didn't press. He had enough to nail Jordan, Eli, and Dr. Tanberg for breach of confidentiality at this point—if not legally, at least, well... by other means. Bruce Tanberg's practice was imploding with every sentence Mel uttered. Craig wondered if, wherever the quack was this evening, he could sense something was about to go down... or if he was out revving engines with Underwood and McTilde.

But Craig wanted more than to shut down a psych practice. He wanted negligence charges brought against everyone involved in the shootings. Proctor Alliance and its subsidiaries. Eli. Underwood, too, if for no other reason than being the biggest patsy in the history of forever.

And Jordan Proctor? He wanted that man to burn.

Craig so badly wanted to feel something for Mel as she sat beside him in this cold, empty building. But he could only nod and process each little bit. He felt hollow—but far from heartless. He'd never known the depth of how badly their breakup had affected her. He and Emma had spoken of it often in their early years.

"Do you regret your choice?" Emma'd asked.

Never. "Never."

"She's got to be devastated to lose such a catch like you."

Though Emma would occasionally jibe him like this, he knew he'd hurt Mel. It was all over her face when he'd broken the news. It was all over her face that first night in The Sicilian, if he were to be honest. That she'd had the guts to enlist him in this mess of a journey was no small miracle. The irony was that she probably found the courage partly due to her work with Tanberg.

Now that healthcare professional had completely shattered Mel's fragile trust. It's highly likely Tanberg was the only one she's trusted in the last few years. She'd certainly lost faith in anyone at Blane.

And Eli? Craig had hoped he'd not cringed when she divulged their short-lived dates and the no-go relationship with that jack wad.

When Mel had had enough, and Craig too, for that matter, the pair made their way out of the mausoleum as the caretaker was about to lock up for the night.

He gave Mel a silent ride back to her house, apologizing for Toby's layer of shed and the faint aroma of wet dog that would permeate the vehicle for all of its days. Other than the engine, the only sound was the occasional swish of the wiper whisking snowflakes and the hum of the heater pouring warmth onto their feet.

He pulled up to her curb and put the Jeep in park. He stared straight out at the street ahead, neat little rows of small houses lining each side of the road, some expelling puffs of smoke from chimneys. "Mel, I do need you to do something." He looked her in the face. "It won't be easy."

"Anything." Even with only the streetlight casting a faint glow over her face, he could tell it was blotchy from the cold and crying. A few stray strands of hair fell from under her ball cap.

"Don't call in sick. Trevor will be getting in touch with you tomorrow sometime."

"Okay. I wasn't planning on skip—"

"Mel." He hesitated, making sure she was listening. "I need you to tell Riki you'd be delighted to help with the benefit banquet. Verbally and in an email."

As she widened her eyes, another round of tears trickled down her cheeks. She turned toward her window and wiped her face on the sleeve of her hoodie. Finally, she offered a shaky "Okay."

She reached for the door handle.

"Mel."

She leaned back in her seat. "There's more? It's going from bad to worse, right? This one will be a doozy."

"After Riki, I need you to make another appointment with Tanberg."

She whipped her head back toward him in shock. "Craig, please, please tell me you have—"

"Mel. I have a plan." He put his hand on her knee and gave it a squeeze. He left it there for a moment, a little dazed that he'd even reached across the seat in the first place.

She stiffened, then rested her pinky on his thumb. They sat that way for a few moments before he moved his hand back to the steering wheel slowly.

"I'll do it." She didn't look at him as she slid from the Jeep and fished her keys out of her pocket. Aside from losing Emma, he couldn't remember when he'd felt so adrift. He had to shake it off.

He had work to do.

27

JORDAN HAD NEVER KNOWN the joys of pet ownership. His parents traveled, so he was a boarding school brat, and his wife—God and the glorious George Washington Bridge rest her unfaithful soul—was too busy being a socialite to manage a mutt. Even a tiny one.

He could tell Nate was reluctant to hand over the dog. "Tink was a gift for my daughter's fifth birthday, sir."

"One that she'll have back in no time, all spic and span, courtesy of Uncle Jordan."

Jordan had seen Nate's daughter exactly once in person. One time too many—and not enough to warrant the "uncle" title. All the other glimpses of this child came from the photos Nate would occasionally tack to the dash of the limo. Photos Jordan insisted the driver take down should be hauling anyone other than himself.

"She hates the carrier, but I'll leave it in case you need it." Nate put Tink in Jordan's arms and the carrier at his feet. The dog's eyes bugged out as it watched Nate pull away, leaving Jordan in front of the penthouse doors with the pink leash flapping in the cold breeze.

He'd most certainly need the carrier.

The young daughter had thwarted Nate's job schedule on at least two occasions, a dance recital and then a dental emergency, Jordan figured the girl owed him the tiniest favor for the inconvenience.

Jordan was full up on inconveniences. The change of travel plans because Eli—not to mention that bloat Underwood—can't manage a simple task. The email he received contained the minutes of the meeting he missed in New York. That one would have to be addressed post-haste when this Craig business was done. Proctor Alliance was losing ground in its race to the Fortune 100. His analysts guessed the company had slipped from the 208 spot to 320 in a matter of months.

In those very same months, he'd spent hand-holding Underwood and his blessed Blane Park instead of seeing personally to his Manhattan business.

But the bitterness drove him to stay in Indiana. Month after month...

It was a lot of work to see the color drain from Craig Thompson's face, but the payoff would be worth it.

After an hour in the penthouse with the yapping Yorkie, Jordan was glad he'd never had the pet experience and that his time with Tink would be short-lived. In the first thirty minutes, the dog whizzed on his bathroom floor, jumped all over his leather sofa, and managed to barricade herself in the closet, becoming hopelessly tangled in the stack of defunct prosthetic legs.

"You're an utterly useless creature."

The second thirty minutes, the dog barked incessantly before losing its voice, giving up, or dying in the closet. Jordan wasn't sure.

He left the hairy beast in the closet. It could stay there

until this was over for all he cared. He had no plans to walk the creature—he called the bellman for that and tipped him handsomely. Jordan, gagging at the thought, laid down puppy pads just in case and sat down a water dish. A dead dog wouldn't serve his needs, and he'd have quite an ordeal sourcing another dog.

He supposed he cared after all.

Jordan made three calls. The call to Dr. Thompson's side hustle could have gone better, adding a whole day to Tink's stay. A youthful voice answered. "I've never been to your fine establishment, but I've heard great things. My Yorkie was misbehaving and got herself into quite a mess. Quite a mess. There's no way I can handle her coat on my own." On cue, Tink poked her head from the closet and tilted her ears back. Her smooth blond locks nearly glowed in the natural light pouring through the wall of windows in Jordan's master suite.

"Do you know what she got into so I can have an idea of how to prepare?"

Jordan hesitated. "No. No idea, but it's a disaster. A real disaster. Would take a groomer with quite a bit of experience if you ask me. How long have you been in this line of work?"

There was a pause. Jordan smiled. He already knew the answer because Jordan did his homework. This kid was the emergency replacement Craig hired to watch the shop while the good doctor went snooping at Blane. Two can play spy games, doc. Two can play.

Where Eli went in unhinged, drawing swings and making a complete mess of things with his chaos, Jordan preferred to play a slower, longer game. An unseen nudge here. A property buyout there. An upgraded lock system to have the keys to any property under Proctor Alliance's umbrella... But Eli set things in motion much too quickly, and now Jordan must adjust.

And adjustment was something Jordan excelled at. It's how he kept Proctor—and Blane, for that matter—on the maps and heading uphill. Time to end this Craig distraction, though. That slip in the Fortune list is bothersome, indeed.

"I assure you, sir, Wagz can handle whatever your pup can throw at us."

Nice answer. "Still, I must insist on the groomer with the most experience."

Another pause. "In that case, sir, you can bring your dog in Saturday. The owner will be here."

Jordan silently screamed at the wait period, but he secured the appointment. He supposed waiting one more day would be worth it to ensure Craig would be on the premises. Jordan could finally have the confrontation he needed to face the man who triaged his leg right into the incinerator.

And if he could land some blows to the useless doggie salon at the same time, so much the better.

His second call was to the maid service, and he was promptly put on hold. This irritated him, but he grabbed his Bluetooth and multitasked while the zippy music played in the background. He rummaged under the bathroom sink but couldn't find anything that he believed would warrant a "real disaster"—at least not without blinding or outright killing the dog.

Once a human operator bothered to give him any attention, he scheduled a thorough cleansing of his whole penthouse to be done as soon as he left with Tink for Wagz. And yes, he'd be happy to pay extra for the weekend service.

He wasn't a monster, after all.

He searched through a couple more closets, contemplating and then dismissing one mess of an idea after another. In the kitchen cabinet, he found the solution. "Hey, Tink, Tink. I know what's on the menu this weekend..."

The third call was to a car service. It wouldn't do to have Nate drive him Saturday, after all. Jordan would let Nate relax with his brat kid while he and Tink took care of long-awaited business.

Another day would give him time to think things through a little more.

Time to decide whether to just pull the plug on Craig's precious Wagz altogether. After all, Proctor Alliance held the deed to many Bella Square properties.

He pulled out his wallet and fished out the slim key card. The master that coded to all of Proctor Alliance's doors.

There were so many doors.

Wagz was one.

Another plan lifted directly from that key card and floated in his vision in a whisp. A better one.

He called back the car service and ordered an earlier pick-up time. A much earlier one.

Had he not been so blinded by his anger, he'd have thought of it earlier, but for this, he would forgive himself.

Dr. Thompson would be crushed. Little by little at first.

Then in a flash. Like a tibia in a motor vehicle accident.

28

Gloves on hands this time around, Mel stood to the side of the HR Courtyard entrance doors, bounced up and down on the balls of her feet, and pulled her coat tighter. The wind whipped this way and that, but the snow flurries had held off so far. Her Uber pulled up, and she tipped the guy extra if he'd idle the car for a few minutes longer.

The bag on her shoulder was cutting off the circulation to her right hand and the sense to her brain. If anyone asked what was in there... why she had the items. She had a story ready, but it was shaky. The Caring Hands Banquet was so important, she wanted to double-check the security badges and clearance. Really, she just wanted Trevor to show up so she could dump all the stuff at Wagz and be done with it.

The security camera above the door blinked an even red eye at her. On and off. On and off. Like it knew what she'd been up to.

Maybe it did.

Where was Trevor?

All day, badge problems, security door issues. This upgrade went as poorly as the last one. The great and mighty Proctor Alliance and Blane Park partnership was again running at its finest, making more work for employees —and worse—putting patients at risk with all the buggy software.

She had a horrid time trying to concentrate on those tasks. Emails flooding in about budgets. She'd fired off a quick "I'll be happy to help do whatever you need for the Caring Hands Banquet" to Riki first thing this morning, so she was fielding tasks for something she wanted no part of. Something that would've sent her spinning off to Dr. T's office for a "squeeze me in, please" session.

C'mon, Trevor...

The Uber driver tilted his head at her, and she PayPal'ed him another five bucks. He turned his head toward his phone, nodded and rested back against his seat.

She so needed a car of her own.

Yesterday evening played on an eternal loop in her head. How much she told Craig. What he asked her to do. Go to work. Work the banquet. Call Tanberg. It was exactly the disaster she'd thought it would be before she ever arrived outside the mortuary. Worse.

The HR doors opened, and Trevor wrestled the cleaning cart over the threshold.

On the bottom shelf was a square black duffel with a large, gold N embroidered on the side. "If anyone asks, you called me about the trash can spill."

"What trash can spill?"

Trevor gave a firm, quick roundhouse to the garbage can at the entrance and grinned, nodding at the cart. "Grab it and go."

Styrofoam cups and paper and fast-food bags blew all over. Startled, Mel glanced up at the camera. Its red eye was dark—no blinking. She shook off the panic and picked up a few pieces of garbage as Trevor righted the can. She reached under the cart, took the duffel, and headed for the impatient Uber. Her hands shook like she'd just robbed the 7-Eleven.

"Good luck, girl! Oh... Oh... And if anyone from security asks," Trevor looked behind his back at the building before laughing out, "We made out!"

Mortified at the implication, she whipped around in all directions to see if they were alone. They were.

And that the little red light remained off. It was.

Trevor whistled as he chased down the rest of the garbage, a spring in his step despite the cold—and despite the fact he just committed a crime.

She slid into the back seat and sat the bag next to her feet. She asked the Uber driver to take the turns carefully and earned a stern eye roll through the rearview mirror. She feared the duffle would slide or the contents would topple the fragile pieces of equipment inside.

Fragile as in sophisticated.

Fragile as in faulty.

Hands still shaking, she pulled out her phone and went to her favorites list. Still only one name in that slot.

Mel: *Spinning out. Need an in-person. Do you have room tomorrow?*

Before she could even rest the phone on her lap, he responded.

Dr. T.: *Anything for you, Mel. Come first thing in the morning.*

29

Trevor came through. When Craig had called the night before with the biggest ask ever, he was all in. Go Navy!

"Happy to cash in on my likability." He belly laughed. "All it took was a pot of my curl-your-chest-hair special roast coffee, and Danishes. I take those Danishes everywhere I need to get something done. And Oscar is easily bought."

Trevor had rolled his utility cart to the basement, clamored around under the eyes in the sky, loading it up with various parts and tools to add to his cover, and, after schmoozing the security guys in the monitor room with high octane coffee and sweets, he waved up at the camera. "I didn't have to wait too long. Oscar loved the Danish. Won't sleep for a week. After that, I figured they'd pay me less attention, if any. Then I honed in on the target." The target being the retired weapons detection scanners stored in the basement.

Craig hoped after all this trouble that they were the same models in use during at least one of the shootings. Both the old and new models were meant to be hidden discreetly inside a planter or trash can. It keeps the aesthetics of a space intact and allows for continual remote monitoring without the need for extra staff. Sounds nice in theory, but...

Trevor had made quick work of the mission and managed to extricate two scanners, slide them into black trash bags and disguise them on his utility cart. Once on the main floor, he'd taken his time to further mask any suspicion he may have aroused. He saw to a spill in the lab and even made quick repair of an overhead light before heading to the locker room, where he slid the scanners into his gym bag.

He passed the gym bag off to Mel at the Courtyard entrance without a hitch. "That took a bit of finagling. But after loading up on my special brew, Oscar believed I was a hound dog and flipped the camera off out there."

"Hound dog?"

"You'll have to ask your girl."

Craig winced. Mel wasn't his girl, but he let that go. Craig had never heard Trevor gloat in all his time working at Blane. "Best time ever. And anything for Emma."

By the time he was off the phone, Mel's Uber had pulled into the spot outside Wagz. She wrestled the bag from the back seat and said something to the driver. The car stayed put.

Craig met her outside and took the duffel. "Good work, Mel."

"Yeah. The security team thinks I'm having a fling with Trevor."

Craig couldn't hide his smile. "I can give you a ride home. We're talking—"

She shook her head. "I can't stay. I have an appointment

with Tanberg in the morning. Just text me what you want me to do."

Craig knew she could stay—she just didn't want to face him. She barely made eye contact with him, and he'd never seen her affect so flat. After all she told him last night, he couldn't blame her. "Thanks. I'll let you know later what we need to tell him."

"What *I* need to tell him. This is my mess. I have to face that narcissistic ass alone."

"Not for long, though. It's almost over. One way or another." Craig shifted the duffel as the Uber honked.

Mel nodded and turned to get in the car. Craig could almost touch the space she left on the sidewalk. He toyed with his thumb—the same one she'd rested her finger on the night before. He breathed in a deep, cold breath and went back inside the salon.

Shake it off.

In 24 hours, the "team" grew from Mel and Craig to include Trevor, Brian, and the latest member—Rhett. Craig could have never guessed this would involve anyone other than him and Mel. He just wanted to gather info enough to get a lawyer to bite and be done with the whole mess. But the longer he studied the wall in his bungalow, the more he was convinced he'd have to force their hand. The shootings and the tie-ins to the security flaws were just too circumstantial.

The same conclusion the legal teams came to. Proctor Alliance had, after all, upgraded the software and fixed the glitches. Blane bought the new system. And no one could prove the glitches were to blame in the first place.

As Craig nutshelled the problem, Rhett hung on his every word. "I know folks affected by this. Most of Indy does. Dad golfed with one of the guys that was shot at that banquet. I'll do whatever you need, Craig."

By late evening, Craig had briefed Brian and Rhett on what Mel had collected, the events at Blane with Underwood and Eli, and a very superficial explanation of Tanberg's involvement—keeping as much of Mel's confession in confidence. She deserved that discretion. He'd yanked the evidence off his living room wall and recreated the setup on the salon office wall.

As much as Craig wanted to disclose his connection to Jordan, he kept that bit close to the vest. He'd tell Mel eventually, but for right now, the group had more important matters than what transpired between Dr. Thompson of eight years ago and his car crash victim he handed off to Dr. McTilde.

Craig had already checked the serial numbers on the hardware against the invoices in Mel's paperwork. They matched two shootings: Blane Dialysis Center and Trauma Bay Two. Craig felt a knot grow in his throat. He was staring straight at the reason Emma didn't stand a better chance that day—

Rhett stared at the papers hanging on the wall. "Proctor Alliance is the same as Jordan, basically? Jordan Proctor's bringing his dog on Saturday. Called this morning. Wanted you, personally, by the sounds of it."

"Jordan Proctor has a dog?" Craig asked. Jordan certainly didn't seem like the type of man that would care for anything but himself. A dog seemed... out of character.

"A Yorkie. Said he'd prefer to have the most experienced groomer on the job."

Brian moaned and Craig seethed. "Of course he does. Rhett, I'm not sure how this will play out. If you don't want to be a part of things—"

"Dude. You guys gave me a huge chance to get out of my parents' basement and away from Mom's nagging. Anything that keeps me away from home long enough for me to afford a place of my own, I'm in. And, you know, for all those folks that died." Rhett crossed his arms and leaned against the wall, staring at the gym bag. "You know, Wagz could use a couple of big planters at the front door. Green things up a bit. We could test it right here. See if the metal on the dog leashes set things off. See if Diane's bling sets it off."

"See if Jordan's leg sets it off," Brian pointed out.

Craig's mind raced. The kid had a point. Wagz could be the testing ground to make sure his rag-tag team could pull off a bigger sting at the banquet.

"It's one thing to have the hardware in front of us. Without the software platform to run it on, we won't know if it'll even do what we need it to do," Rhett said. "Professional gaming was my next vocation choice, but I doubt that's what we're dealing with."

"Glad we got you outta the basement." Brian cradled his sling a little closer and leaned on the wall beside Rhett. Craig sank into his office chair, Toby on one side, Hackett on the other. A true meeting of the minds. The clock above Craig's desk ticked off the seconds, everyone racking their brains.

"Clarence." Craig grinned. "Didn't he say something about hacking?"

"I know he said something about coke and hookers. But yeah. I think in the middle of white-hot pain, I do recall him alluding to some untoward hobbies."

Tomorrow is Friday. Jordan is Saturday, and Sunday is the Caring Hands Banquet. "Can we pull this off in three days?" He'd need Mel to be on her game, and he just didn't know if he could count on her to hold it together that long. She'd been so hurt...

"I'll pitch this to Clarence, see if he can score the software, run the test. Mel is helping set up the venue."

"That's unfortunate," Brian said, then backed it up. "You said she feels responsible for the banquet shooting. Now again? Another one?"

Craig rubbed his hands through his hair. "Yeah. She's going to have it rough, but she'll be okay."

I hope.

"If the hearing aid guy can steal weapons detection software as easily as we hope he can, we've got a much, much bigger problem," Rhett pointed out.

Craig brightened and his heart raced. They were so close now. "You mean *Proctor Alliance* has a much bigger problem. If Clarence can do it... that could be the smoking gun we need to put them out of business, even if we don't get a direct correlation to the shootings. We can put an end to the company that employed the system to begin with."

The system ran on Proctor's proprietary software. And Craig was banking that Jordan didn't hire the best and the brightest, only the slightly competent at the lowest bid.

"And Brian?"

"Yeah, boss."

"Invite every police officer your brother ever knew to that banquet. Every last one. I'll have Mel throw in a First Responder recognition of some sort. Alfred won't be able to resist it." Craig bent down and gave Hackett a scratch behind the ears. "Ready to go back to active duty, boy?"

Hackett tipped his head in typical shepherd fashion and held Craig's gaze.

Hackett, indeed, was ready.

Now Craig just needed to prep Melody for tomorrow's therapy appointment.

30

MEL SPLASHED cold water over her face before her appointment. The late-night chat with Craig brought her little peace. She still wasn't sure what the whole plan was— wasn't sure she wanted to know. It did irk her, though, that she'd bared all to Craig, and he was clearly holding more cards than he was showing.

Maybe he didn't trust her to not spill vital information to Dr. T.

She couldn't say she'd blame him there.

She dried her face off, avoiding the mirror—the one in her bathroom this morning told her all she needed to know. Dark circles barely covered by foundation and a tenseness across her jawline that will surely cause a migraine-level headache sooner or later.

She paused at the bathroom door.

One foot in front of the other and chin up, girl. As difficult as this appointment will be, being on point at the banquet Sunday would be even harder. Eli and Dr. T would be there. And her boss.

And Craig.

If she concentrated, she could still feel the warmth of his hand resting on her knee when he dropped her off the other night...

Not now, Mel. Concentrate.

At least Craig would have security covered at this event. She'd already emailed Riki and Alfred the all-important addition of a thank you for first responders. In addition to firefighters and EMS, several police officers and their K-9s would be in attendance. The likelihood of any repeat of the Vanderbilt locale was slim to none.

Alfred took that opportunity, hook, line, and sinker. Even put out a notice to the papers and bloggers about the high regard Blane holds these folks in. Underwood was never one to lose out on a media plug.

Now, all Mel had to do was drop in a few lines during the session that she'd found a thread connecting Proctor Alliance with the faulty software. She was going to be in contact with Blane's legal team later today. All good since the banquet was two days away and all.

So easy.

Just some little white lies. Something she'd never done with Dr. T. Not once. Why would you when you trusted that the person in front of you could help navigate the darkest storms of your life?

Craig created the bait in hopes that an actual communication thread between Eli, Underwood, and Dr. T. would emerge. Irrefutable proof of the three cohorts in action. Craig seemed to have worked it out, just like he'd promised. A plan and all...

She arrived a few minutes early at the waiting area, and before she could sit, Dr. T's secretary waved her into the room. "He'll be in shortly. He's on a call with another patient."

Mel smiled and went into the all-too-familiar space. Black couch that didn't recline. His chair did. Desk in the corner that he never sat behind while she was there.

The photos.

She bypassed the couch, went for the photo with the Mercedes, and picked up the frame. The passengers. She'd not looked so closely before. From her spot on the couch, the faces were blurry, and it wasn't her business what Doc did in his free time.

But now she could see clearly.

Alfred. Eli.

And Jordan Proctor.

If Craig knew about this, he'd left that name out of the plan. Three cohorts. Not four? Her mind spun, and she felt that all-too-familiar sense of betrayal creep around her ribs.

"Good morning, Mel."

She jumped and bobbled the frame to his desk.

"Mel? Something up?" He reached around her and righted the picture.

She backed up and slid onto the couch, feeling the blood drain from her face. "I, uh..." The whole plan had fallen out of her head as quickly as the frame had fallen from her fingers. *Think, Mel. Think.*

"Yeah, Dr. T. I want out. Out of all of it."

31

Nine days ago, Craig Thompson was a simple dog groomer worried about the bubble art on the turquoise walls. After unknowingly making enemies of the most powerful businessmen this side of the Mississippi, Craig was ring-leading a precarious sting operation with the most misfit team of "experts" ever known to man.

But the more he got to know Rhett, Brian—and even Clarence—the more he understood how much he'd been missing in his life since Emma passed.

Connection.

After Emma, there was no social life. There was barely a life outside Toby and the brief interaction with the humans dropping off hounds at Wagz. He'd been starving himself of friendships. Now he had this grieving real estate agent and Clarence with all his oddities. Rhett, too. It felt... right.

Craig and the gang stayed at the Bella Square Strip Mall well after their respective closing times Friday to discuss the plan.

Proctor Alliance was the target. Not Blane Park. Alfred may be on the take and would probably lose his job, but Craig had no interest in shutting down a major medical provider—it provided too many people with life-saving interventions. All those patients waiting on treatments and tests. Those that come through the trauma bays. No, Blane Park, for all the flaws of its captain, had to remain as intact as possible. With upgraded security, that is, but still operational.

For Mel, the biggest target was Tanberg, but they would have enough on him, Eli, and even Underwood's involvement to take those fools down so long as Mel's therapy appointment this morning went as planned.

A nagging tug started in his stomach. She'd not answered his calls or texts, but that was understandable. Mel was surely swamped with the plans for the banquet— and he had thrown another responsibility on her with the police officers attending.

While they waited for Rhett to bring back food, he poked his head back into the lobby of Wagz and inspected the entryway. Again. Two large planters—courtesy of Emma's collection—housed the security scanners on either side of the entry door. Clarence configured them for a test run tomorrow for when Jordan comes through. Officer Rigley was on the books to bring in Ava, a nothing-but-muscle-and-teeth Malinois model, for a spa day. After Brian gave Zoe a quick run-down, she gladly offered her services, off duty, of course. A true test-run of the system since she'd be packing, no doubt.

Clarence would utilize the empty space next to Wagz to monitor the software and adjust the sensitivity. Turns out Clarence augmented his impeccable computer savvy with his expert-level locksmithing. The audiologist showed off these skills and set up the monitors in the next retail space. "You won't even know I'm there."

Brian's face went pale, and he just shook his head. "I can't believe I'm doing this with you guys, man." Craig gave him a gentle pat on the back. Rhett came back with large pizzas and a larger smile.

"Let me guess. A girl?" Clarence said.

Rhett shrugged and went red in the face. The waitress the kid described sounded a lot like Sadie.

"You get her number?"

"No, not yet."

"Whatcha waitin' for? Need me to intervene? I got some skills in that—"

Rhett cut Clarence short. "No, no. I'll handle it."

The guys chowed down and went over and over the plan. Clarence assured them he could score the additional cabling and gadgetry required to piggyback onto the banquet's security system feed. He already had most of it in his "stash." Craig didn't ask, and Rhett just shook his head. Brian pretended not to care, but he fidgeted with his sling a little more than was necessary. Craig could see visions of jail cells floating over Brian's head.

After going over the game plan a dozen times, Craig instructed Brian and Rhett to take down the wall and store the documents in Brian's safe next door. He walked Clarence to the parking lot.

"I've got another, uh... favor. I'd do it myself, but I think you'd be faster."

"Keepin' me hoppin', doc. Glad it's the weekend." Clarence slid into his sedan, leaving the door open. "Whatcha need?"

Craig pulled a notecard from his back pocket with two names scribbled in red ink. "Can you look into these people? They're deceased. I want to know if they had any connection to each other before… well. The timeframe would be eight years ago, maybe even as far back as ten."

Clarence took the card and nodded. "Stalkin' the dead, now. There's a story here."

"Yeah. One that I don't want the rest of the gang to know about yet. You okay with that?"

He grinned and took the duffel from Craig. "As long as you got me that immunity from all of Brian's buddies in blue, I'm okay with just about anything." He strained to pull the bag across his lap and into the passenger seat and rubbed his neck.

"Brian assured us. Rigley was his brother's partner. They're tight. Just keep a low profile." Craig couldn't help himself. He leaned against the driver's door, unable to turn off the internal diagnostician, and nodded toward Clarence's shoulder. "Looks sore. You been walking Hackett?"

"No, no. That dog hates me since the treats dried up. I've been working out." Clarence grinned up from behind the steering wheel, flexed his left biceps, and grasped his chest. "Now I'm a little lopsided."

Ever the doctor, Craig said, "You need a trainer. Someone to show you proper technique so you don't hurt yourself."

"No kidding. Only my left tit grew and now I can't swing a golf club without jacking up my shoulder. I feel for Brian."

Craig guffawed and leaned his head on top of the car. "Seriously, Clarence. Get help."

"Will do. Will do. Hey… when I get all situated up at the party, you think I can hide down in the drainpipes like the hackers do in the movies?"

Craig stepped away from the car and stepped back. "Better leave the manhole covers closed. Stick with the plan."

Clarence shrugged. "You got it, Doc." He drove away, and as his sedan disappeared into Bella Square, Craig's heart rate rose. Time was ticking away. Soon, either they'd be successful at stopping Jordan, quietly and without sacrificing patient care—or they'd all be in jail at the mercy of Hackett's former coworkers.

Another tug from under his ribs prompted him to fish out his phone. No notifications.

Why hadn't he heard from Mel?

32

Jordan put the carrier on the front seat next to the driver. He'd had quite enough of the impossible Yorkie and Jordan had no intentions of sharing the back seat with her. The one-off driver gave him a look, but Jordan handed him a fifty and the look disappeared.

He also issued the driver the same stern warning about watching the roads. Friday night gifted Indianapolis with yet another quick coat of snow, and since it's the weekend, who knows what kind of replacements would be out plowing, if any. And not before the sun was all the way up on a weekend.

Weekends. Jordan knew no weekend. No one else should either.

He supposed he needed to forgive folks for needing a break. But those folks won't get to the top. Reaching the kinds of heights he had in mind for Proctor Alliance didn't come if you took a break.

This whole ordeal with Blane Park and its pathetic Underwood, and now the side trek with Dr. Thompson, has proved that. Falling in the Fortune 100. How could he have let this happen?

Revenge, Jordan. You want revenge.

Petty? Maybe. He adjusted the pantleg crease around his prosthetic.

No. Not petty. Craig's fall would be the emotional and mental boost Jordan needed to finally put the ordeal behind him and focus solely on launching Proctor Alliance to heights unknown. It'll be the most epic rise the business world has ever seen.

Time Magazine.

Forbes.

They'd all be lining up for interviews and "tell me how you did it."

Jordan would never be able to tell them just how. That started with freeing himself of Evan and Angie.

But the rest? He'd talk about tenacity and perseverance and a relentless drive for success.

That stuff sold articles and launched statuses.

The driver pulled in front of Wagz. "Hold here. Not sure how long I'll be."

Jordan maneuvered the carrier from the front seat, fished the keycard from the jacket pocket, and faced the strip mall. Pathetic little four-spot, one of them empty. The previous property owners clearly showed no promise. No wonder they were so easily bought out.

Proctor Alliance's subsidiaries promptly changed all the locks on the doors with key slides. Of course, each business had its own code and keyed entry. But Jordan held the master.

He slid the card through the reader, and with a satisfying digital beep, the deadbolt retreated into the door and allowed him entry to his building.

"Oh, Dr. Thompson, what have you done with the place?" Gut-wrenching stench and the most ridiculous décor greeted him. Poorly painted walls. Sparse products on the shelves. Unnecessarily large planters guarded the door, hindering maneuverability. He imagined the male dogs wouldn't be able to resist hiking a leg on them. Jordan made a mental note to never own a dog and never fall for anyone that wanted one.

He sat Tink's carrier down and gave it a slight kick away from him, the plastic sliding over the slick concrete. He took a quick look around the place as he twirled the keycard in his fingers. Bathing stations, office, small back room.

He removed his jacket and draped it over the front counter. Tink yapped from the carrier, but he ignored her. He leaned against the hideous blue paint, his weight on his real leg, the other propped against the wall.

Then Jordan waited for the owner to show up for work.

33

Hyped up on energy drinks since he'd been asked to join Craig on this little sting, Clarence texted before the sun was up.

Clarence: *This is why you use the manholes, man.*
This is why the manholes.

Craig, not alert yet given the late night and the worry over no word from Mel, called Clarence. That didn't go much better than trying to decipher the text.

Toby rolled over in the bed next to him with a moan, throwing his front paws over Craig's throat. Craig moved them down and rubbed Toby's head as Clarence went on.

"The system is online. I went back after y'all left and tinkered with it. Left the old software running on one scanner. Installed, well, I improved and then installed my own version on the second. Had the info sent to my phone and all. No biggie. Just took a minute..."

Craig still wasn't fully awake. "What are you getting at?"

"Man. Get with it. A titanium body part is in your shop right now. Unless someone else with one leg has a grudge against you, I'm guessing it's that Proctor guy. Thought you should know."

Now Craig was awake.

"Jordan's in my shop?"

"Well, it's his real estate."

"He's trespassing."

"Man, you don't read much, do you? They've got the keys. We signed the lease. They have a master. When did you open that store, anyway? Don't you remember them switching out for digital locks? At first, I was like, cool. An upgrade. Then I was like, wait. Digital can be hacked. I should know. Then I was like—"

He let Clarence's rant fall into the background. Craig was in such a grieving funk when he signed the lease on the storefront. He was in a funk when he buried Emma in a spot he could never be. He was in a funk in his bungalow and... Of course, he remembered them changing the locks, but it happened so quickly after he started Wagz—even before the first pooch showed up for a bath.

His heart sank. He jumped out of bed, startling Toby to do the same and let out a bark.

Right after he signed the lease.

Before his first dollar was made.

How long has Jordan been after him? Watching? This is stalker-level...

"—I even tried. I mean, I never tried, tried to get into Rivers or Wagz, but I did the empty one next to us. That's how I got in the other night so quickly. I'd already hacked it once."

"Wait. Wait. Back up a minute." Craig's mind was working awake.

"You tweaked it for titanium? So it works, like really well?"

He could nearly hear Clarence's smile bust open right over the phone. "Yeah, man. Tweaked it for all metals. Not hard. Not hard at all. Top-line stuff. My software upgrades are top-of-the-line, that is. The stuff you brought me? The scanners, the hardware, are legit. But the code they're running right now? Man, I wouldn't trust it to watch over a pile of dog sh—" He caught himself. "I'm just sayin', Doc, my talent is wasted most days. I mean, I help really old folks hear and all that, and they think I'm a genius. But this other is my wheelhouse, man. This is where—"

"Clarence, slow down." Craig's mind raced and his pulse pounded as he pulled on jeans and a T-shirt and leashed Toby. "Did you get that other thing looked into? Those names?"

"Check your email, Doc. When you gonna see I'm a miracle worker?"

"Thanks." He hung up and flung open the laptop.

Clicked open the files from Clarence.

The audiologist really was a miracle worker.

And Jordan Proctor is a dead man walking.

34

Mel's guilt over going rogue in the therapy appointment kept her up all night. Yet another thing she'd have dealt with in therapy. The irony of all this kicked at her, but the dominos were toppling now, and there was nothing she could do to stop them.

She opened her bedroom curtains, allowing the dim morning light to flow in. A fresh layer of flakes greeted her. She opened the window just a crack and let the freezing air wash over her. Omega came running, eager to get a sniff of the outdoors.

She'd thought about calling Craig yesterday—more than once—but he clearly had a side quest that she had no information on.

Again, with the irony, given what she held from him. But she couldn't help wondering if he even cared what Eli and Tanberg did to her. She wasn't sure about Underwood —where he fit, other than he loved the limelight and to be admired. At any rate, she would never work for Blane Park again. She'd see to her duties Sunday to keep her promise to

Craig, then turn in her badge to Linda and turn her back on the whole mess. Pack up Omega. Her books.

A few bottles of wine.

And start over somewhere else. Somewhere not Indiana.

Florida? No. She loved the snow.

Minnesota, maybe. She and Omega would start over in Minnesota. A cabin. Quiet. No investigations or fighting or banquets or therapists.

She went to her closet and slid hangers around until she unearthed her black dress. The dress she would've worn to the Vanderbilt disaster had she not chickened out because Eli would be in attendance that night. Another stab of the irony knife.

She shook the hanger, allowing the fabric to breathe. Had she been present for that shooting, she may have had a full-blown mental break.

You picked the venue. You picked Sunday's, too.

She shook off the intrusive thought. Craig had security under control already... and though he dumped her and held her in the dark, she believed he had that part under control.

Now, she had the opportunity to slide into it tomorrow night. Bling it up with a little cubic zirconia here and there and stick it to Tanberg and Eli once and for all.

Craig can do his thing—she knew he needed to for Emma's sake and his own.

But she'd do hers.

The men in her life had let her down. Kept her in the dark. Hurt her. One after the other after the other. Over and over.

Omega brushed up against her leg. She reached down to pet him. "You're the only one for me, demon cat. The only one." He nipped at her hand then flung his tail in her face.

Yup. Every single male in her life.

She stood and held the dress out at arm's length. It was time to stop the cycle of dependence. Time to stand on her own and take back her power...

If she ever had any to begin with.

35

CRAIG CAME up with and promptly discarded a dozen ways to confront Jordan's intrusion. Park the Jeep four blocks away and sneak in the back.

Simply don't show up.

Drive the Jeep through the front door.

Each idea became more and more ridiculous and based in pure rage.

Clearly, none of them would produce the desired result —to take Jordan down and remain as above board as possible (already tainted because of the medical files snooping and involving what turned out to be a world-class hacker in this mess).

And to honor Emma.

What would you do, Em? I just can't see it.

"What would Emma do, Toby?" He wasn't even sure he should've brought the dog. He'd leashed the lab and put him in the Jeep out of pure muscle memory more than anything else.

Emma'd found herself in a complicated mess with an

unruly boss at Mount Lombard in their earliest days on duty in Manhattan.

"If you stay quiet and smile, eventually, evil can't stand it. It just starts showing off."

Stay quiet. Maybe he could do that.

Smile? No way. Not for the likes of Jordan.

He parked in the back lot. Fished out the key to the back door, and entered, just like he would on any other day. Led Toby down the hall to his office, but before he could dump his keys and coat in the office, Toby's hackles rose, and a low growl emitted from deep in his chest.

"Is someone here?" Best to play it dumb.

Dumb he could do. Smiling no.

No answer. Toby's growl intensified.

The files Craig sent burned a hole in his mind. Evan. Angela. Those deaths from the George Washington Bridge are linked to Jordan, Craig just knew it, but like the links to the faulty software, he lacked just a few more strings to tie it all in a nice bow.

He so much wanted to put his hands on the man, the red closing in like the day in the ER with Eli. And that didn't go well.

Craig flipped on the light switch next to Emma's photo. He leaned his forehead against the wall next to her, willing her voice to fill his head. Longed to feel her touch on his cheek. The brush of her hand...

Breathe. Stay quiet. Play dumb. In Emma's voice. *Smile.*

Like hell I'm smiling about this, and neither will you. He startled. That voice wasn't Emma's.

That was straight up Mel. He was losing his mind. His pulse galloping at an all-time high.

"Hello?" Craig tried again to get Jordan to answer

before he had a problem with Toby and became even more distracted.

Whining and a few yaps echoed down the hall. Toby pulled harder.

He wound Toby's leash around his hand a little tighter. "Heel, boy." The dog obeyed, but remained vocal until they encountered a carrier. The whining from inside crescendoed, then settled. Toby's tail wagged for a split second at the creature inside, but then he looked beyond again to the entry.

The pair entered the foyer, Craig flipping on the lights as he went. Jordan, impeccably dressed for a Saturday, tailored suit and all, leaned against the wall. Toby lunged, Craig corrected him with a jerk to the leash, took the dog to the front of the counter and tied him to the holding hook.

"About time you got here, Dr. Thompson. Or is it simply Craig in this setting? These things can be so difficult to sort out."

"How'd you get in here?" Craig hesitated, then added, "And who are you?"

"No need to play it that way, Craig. You know who I am. After all, you never forget a patient, do you? That's the word from your counterpart, anyway. Eli's been a great source of information." He picked at his nails. "Most days, anyway."

"How'd you get in here?" Play dumb, but not too dumb.

"Oh, I own this." Jordan waved his arms wide. He stood away from the wall and moved toward Toby, who was in an uncharacteristic state, with a growl that wouldn't end, gasping every few seconds to hold enough oxygen in his lungs to keep it going. "But you must know that by now, right? All the gumshoe detective work you've been up to."

Craig said nothing.

"I'm closing this down. Your precious Wagz. How'd you say it back in your days of trauma work? Triage? The most important things first? Well, Dr. Thompson, for eight years the most important thing in my life has been to see you fall."

"You'll have to explain that to me. I've done nothing to you."

"Ha! That's the truth. You passed me off as a dead man to Eli. Sub-par skills." He tapped his leg. "Sub-par limb."

"Look, that's nothing—" Craig stopped himself. He owed this monster no apology or explanation. Stay quiet. Let evil show its hand.

Jordan's phone buzzed and he fished it out. Grinned. "Looks like your girl got cold feet. If you were depending on her involvement to take Proctor Alliance by storm, you'll have to find someone more competent. The meek shall inherit the earth is nothing but a bold-faced lie."

A bell and the sound of Rivers Realty's back door slamming meant Brian had arrived. Craig prayed he'd stay over there—or that Clarence had given him the heads up. Hackett barked. A low, deep woof. Toby's growl hit a new level. More whining from the carrier.

Jordan pocketed his phone and slung his coat on. "It's folks like us. Folks who can make the split-second decisions between life and death. The life and death of a business. Of an entire hospital that's the blood suck of a corporation. Of patients and their abilities to make livelihoods."

Craig's blood boiled. *Quiet. Calm.* Emma's ghost again.

Hackett's racket hit an all-time high. Toby's voice was becoming hoarse, drool hanging from his jowls.

Jordan reached the door. "Poor Emma. You think she'd be proud of this?" He threw a hand to the wall Craig had doodled on. "She'd roll over in her grave."

Walls of red threatened to take over Craig's vision until

he spotted a patrol car pull up behind the black sedan parked on the street that Jordan must've arrived in.

Officer Rigley. Ava. They were seconds from reaching the door. Ava's fur was up, head cocked to the side, first toward Rivers, then toward Wagz. The Malinois was on high alert. And Jordan noticed.

"Best officially unlock for business. Make a few more bucks while you can. God knows you won't be working here for long. Here or in medicine. Ever."

Jordan opened the door, setting off the chime. He stepped out to the sidewalk, snow swirling around him, flakes falling inside. He held the door open for Rigley and Ava, keeping a wide berth between himself and the powerful dog.

"Oh, and you can keep the Yorkie. I won't be needing her."

* * *

"You okay, buddy?" Brian had stayed behind the scenes in his storefront until the sedan pulled away with Jordan in it. The scene in Wagz had settled, and so had the dogs. Toby was on his bed. Hackett was quiet next door, finally. Craig freed the Yorkie from the carrier. He called Rhett in, instructing him to stop by the vet's office first to pick up a microchip reader to see if the dog belonged to someone. It seemed unharmed other than emotionally distraught.

But she was a Yorkie, so it was hard to tell.

Clarence burst through the back door, startling all the dogs again. "Good news, guys! My version of the software knows the difference between legs and lugers—" He stopped mid-sentence when he saw the cop car. And then processed Zoe and Ava's presence. "I mean. Well, lugers, I mean—"

Craig let out a moan. "Cops don't carry lugers."

Officer Rigley smiled.

"You carry a luger?"

"Not on duty." She patted her back. "Was my grand-dad's. It's my backup piece. At least on the weekends." She hung Ava's lead to the hook where Toby had just been and told the dog to settle. Ava did so without hesitation. She looked around the foyer. "Planter scanners?"

Craig nodded.

"This is what I was telling you guys about. We think—we know—Blane is using faulty software provided to them by Proctor Alliance. We just can't tie it all together."

"But it picked up my piece."

Clarence beamed. "That's because I hacked—tweaked, tweaked. I upgraded, I mean."

Craig saved him again. "We have one scanner running on the original software that we believe was in use during the shootings. The other Clarence upgraded."

Craig and Brian took the planters apart to show Zoe. "I'm a fan of using tools for security, but nothing can beat the human element. Use the software for after-hours or unpopulated areas. But always, always have human eyes and boots on the ground where lives are at stake."

"No arguments here."

"Guys! Guys! Is that a Yorkie?" Clarence hit his knees and spread his arms. The long-haired, short-legged little blonde ran to him like she knew him. "I love, love, love you. Yes I do." The dog plastered him with kisses. Clarence rose with the dog in his arms.

"You're just full of surprises, aren't you?" Brian rubbed his shoulder. "Do we need a new plan for the banquet?

Craig slumped against the wall and slid to the floor. "I need to think. Remember exactly what Jordan said. Someone bring me paper and a pen."

Breathe. Think. Move.

He needed to know what Mel did. What that message Jordan got meant. Evil had showed its hand, though. Jordan was out for Craig's reputation *and* career—any career he could get his hands on.

Brian, Clarence, and Zoe waited for him to process. Rhett showed up with the scanner, and Clarence didn't want to hand over the little dog. The chip reader registered a number. "I'll call it in to the vet. But it's Saturday, and the roads are getting bad..." Rhett handed Clarence back the dog.

"I don't think we need a new plan. Mel may be ticked off at me. Who knows what Tanberg fed her. Right now, we need a safe place for Toby and the Yorkie. I don't want to chance that Jordan will come in here and do something to one of them."

"They can hang in the basement. I'll put on a video game replay. Mom'll never know." Rhett bent to love on Toby.

He sent off a rapid 911 text to Mel. No answer.

He tried calling twice with similar results.

Not good. Not good at all. He pushed the fear aside and rose from the floor to get the duffel from the office.

Craig breathed and went over everyone's places for the Caring Hands Banquet. The red in his vision cleared and his pulse calmed as he began to lead his team.

Toby was on unexpected Yorkie-sitting duty. As soon as Clarence let go of the mini yapper, she cuddled right up to Toby on his bed and went to sleep.

Zoe, Ava, and another dozen officers and their K-9s

would hold places of honor. Full dress blues. Underwood couldn't resist the opportunity to show off Blane's community ties and how much the organization loved its first responders. Even the fallen ones: Brian and Hackett will attend in honor of Brian's brother. True to her word, Zoe had brought Hackett a special vest to wear for the evening.

Clarence would make his way to the security room of the venue, the lower-level office suites, courtesy of a badge Mel had stuffed in the duffel before she went radio silent. "Not quite the drainpipe, but close enough."

She'd also scored Rhett a valet attendant's vest and security badge. The kid beamed. "This is gonna rock."

Craig's mood lifted as he looked around his Wagz-turned-sting headquarters. He'd been holding on to the guilt and grief for so long. Tiny hints of blue sky were hard to come by. But this group. This purpose... The connection. It changed the flavor of the grief to something more tolerable.

Alfred Underwood had issued four personal invitations to this banquet. The chief executive officer of Blane Park Medical only remembered issuing three, however: Eli. Bruce. Jordan.

The fourth was tucked in a pristine white envelope with Craig Thompson's name in perfect script. Mel had done fabulously, no matter what she was up to now. He just had to trust her.

Craig would use the invite to waltz into the benefit like he belonged there.

Because he did.

Because Emma needed him to.

Because it was time to move on from all of it.

36

IF THIS WEREN'T such a tense night, it could be a glorious one.

Mel had done a fabulous job securing the location for the Caring Hands Banquet in the shiny new neighborhood of Candle View. He'd breathed a huge sigh of relief when she'd told him it wouldn't be held in Bella Square—way too much happening too close to home these days.

And maybe Proctor Alliance hadn't started noosing the businesses here yet. No one for Jordan to hold a grudge against in Candle View.

Everglow Plaza stretched over a city block's worth of real estate, free-standing banquet centers and ballroom façade made to look like an old-time village lined the edge. In the summer, an impressive water fountain entertained passersby with dancing sprays and lights. Tonight, it was covered over with an equally impressive pre-holiday display, glistening evergreen trees dotted with glowing candles. Lanterns strung above the cobblestone walkways between ornate metal sculpture work swayed gently in the evening's cool breeze. Spits of snow added to the magic.

Magic? He's had too many voices in his head. Too brain fatigued. Magical is a word Emma would've used to describe the plaza, not him.

Or Mel. Mel would describe it as magical.

The snow more accurately reminded him of the thousand doubts and worries he had going into this evening. And those weren't magical at all.

Craig arrived early, avoiding a repeat of Jordan jumping the gun on him like he had yesterday. He handed over the keys to the Jeep and took a lint roller to remove a layer of Toby from his tux before the valet—Rhett—took his truck away to a nearby garage. Clarence had texted him hours ago that things were a go on his end—the scanners, new ones already sourced and placed by Blane Park security and the two old ones Trevor resurrected, were dotted along the entryways, masked in ornate trash receptacles and oversized planters. Clarence assured him the software was running. Three versions: The faulty one, the upgraded one in use in all of Blane's properties this present second, and the version Clarence had tweaked.

Too much reliance on AI is what Officer Rigley had said. Hopefully this little experiment would prove that to be true. Craig was comforted knowing that Brian had wrangled so many officers and their K-9s to arrive interspersed with the other guests. Guests that Alfred and Jordan no doubt hoped would bring with them thousands of dollars in pledges for the next Blane Park expansion.

Craig wondered how much of the profits tonight would be dogeared for Proctor's involvement. Or used to source more sub-par equipment from the sub-par supplier. If Mel would return his calls, maybe she could have shed some light on it.

No use worrying about that detail now...

As Rhett disappeared in the Jeep, Craig breathed the crisp air and smoothed his trousers. The last time he wore this tux was when he and Emma had attended a similar event for Blane after they first moved back to Indiana. When he laid it out last night, he smelled the lapels of the jacket—the place where she'd have laid her head on him when they danced.

No trace of her was left there, though, the clothing having been dry-cleaned and hanging for so long. The seams weren't as tailored to his frame, grief having chipped away at his physique over the years.

He shook off the memory and started looking for a spot to wait and watch before presenting his forged invitation to the banquet's host staff to check in at the biggest building at the end of the plaza where Caring Hands was being held. From the looks of it, that was the only building in use tonight, so he scaled the steps of a smaller hall and leaned in the doorway to watch the valet circle and pray. He reached into his breast pocket and felt for the invitation.

And the nearly worn-out printout he'd created from Clarence's email.

Mel arrived shortly after Craig, and she walked right by him, his black tux helping him to blend in with the doorframe in the subtle light. He resisted the urge to call out to her, ask her if she was okay. Ask her why she was ghosting him. But he said nothing.

Her heels clicked along the cobblestone, and she headed for the far building. Riki, he thought, was on one side of her. Linda on the other.

She was wrapped in a long dress coat and pulled it

tighter as she walked. She paused, allowing her escorts to go ahead. She tipped her head to the sky, the snowflakes falling on her cheeks. He toyed with that thumb again. That place where they'd allowed a moment of connection... He felt his face flush and then jammed his hands deep into his pockets.

Mel righted herself and went on, the trio of ladies fishing out their invitations as they headed down the path.

———

More and more cars arrived. Standard ones. Fancy ones.

Then high-powered ones. Craig perked up.

First Alfred in his Ferrari. Craig watched as Rhett beat another valet to the honor. The kid was having the time of his life. Real-world SIMS game right here.

By the time Underwood made it to the host station, Eli pulled up in his silver Jag. The money just dripped from these people. And at the expense of patient care and people's lives. Craig struggled to remain at his post. It would do no good to make a scene before everyone was inside. Rhett was a little slow on the draw and missed the opportunity to park Eli's.

Mel had told him Bruce Tanberg drove a Mercedes. A couple had pulled up so far, but no one matching Tanberg's staff directory photo climbed out until the fourth coup. Fiery red, enough to emit a glow. No doubt Mel wished he'd burn in that automobile. Craig couldn't blame her.

That was three of the four he was waiting on. Jordan had a driver, but he'd still arrive at the valet spot to be dropped off.

Unless he was already inside and had beaten Craig to the punch again. Craig needed to be sure he was in there before going in. Despite the cold, Craig broke out in a hot sweat.

Breathe, Block, Move.

A deep inhale.

Exhale.

Block out distractions and worries. The other guests. Whether Clarence was behaving. Whether Toby was behaving in Rhett's basement. Whether Rhett would wreck one of those uber expensive rides. Whether the host would take his invite. On and on.

Move.

Get into the venue. Jordan must be inside by now. The officers were arriving in dress blues, their K-9s in their on-duty vests. Police cars lined the street along the Candle View neighborhood for as far as Craig could see. No valet parking those babies. Brian and Hackett rode with Zoe and Ava. Their two police dogs walked shoulder to shoulder, heads held proudly, like they were on a date.

Craig allowed himself a quick smile despite the distress.

Maybe the dogs were dating.

The inflow slowed to a trickle, and for the first time, there was no line at the host stand.

Craig took two steps away from his perch at the door and was about to descend the stairs and blend in with the dwindling crowd on the cobblestones. One last look toward the valet station sent him ducking back to the doorway.

A stretch limo parked.

The driver emerged and went to the back to open the door and wait stalwart while the occupant emerged.

Jordan Proctor. Dead man walking.

Jordan nodded at the driver and quickly buttoned his overcoat as he stepped out of the stretch. The new car service was proving to be sub-par to his personal driver, but he'd rather start over at this point than deal with Nate's whining. He'd get his dog back, eventually. And his little girl could quit her crying.

Craig would see to that, Boy Scout he is.

In the meantime, Nate was given his walking papers and could find another soul to speed around Indy with. Jordan was moving on.

The milieu was quaint. Villages reeked of poverty. Blane couldn't even hold a fundraiser event in a venue worthy of the cause. Melody Atkins had picked the place, no doubt, but the buck stopped with Alfred Underwood. Jordan wanted Mel's involvement, the most weak and timid link in Craig's chain, according to the info Tanberg had fed him.

But wow. Everglow Plaza needed a fundraiser of its own.

Jordan brushed the flakes from his face. And the snow was impossibly annoying. The walkways should've been covered, cobblestone posed a tripping hazard to men like him—well, not quite like him. Men in his position who couldn't afford the level of physical therapy that Jordan had endured. Men like those.

He arrived at the host station, the attendant all dolled up with her blonde hair curled on top of her head and navy dress—matchy-matchy with the Caring Hands logo, no doubt—and dripping with fake ruby bling scanned his invitation and waved him on.

"Welcome, Mr. Proctor. It's a true pleasure to have you tonight. Have a wonderful evening. We hope you'll be blessed beyond—"

"Yeah, yeah." He nodded and stepped inside. He was the keynote speaker once Underwood got done peacocking the crowd. Underwood kept Jordan's on-stage appearance under wraps, only listing "special guest speaker" in the printed materials.

Jordan wasn't in a rush. His spot had been bumped back for the first responder nonsense. First responders fell into the same category as the likes of Craig, in Jordan's opinion. That day on the George Washington could have gone so much differently if people had realized what a fighter he was. That he was worth saving.

He meandered along the exterior hallways to the backstage area. Not much of a greenroom, if you asked him. Quaint, like the venue. Sofa, fruit basket. Wet bar with nothing but water and tonic. At least there was a door to the outside off the backstage hospitality area. No matter that it said Emergency Exit, he popped the door open and was greeted by heavy snowfall and a quick burst of ice-cold air.

The cold Jordan could take. The snow? He hated the snow. At any rate, Jordan would order his new driver around the back of the plaza and make a quick getaway from the fray before people started getting too handsy.

He was certainly glad to have started the ball rolling on Craig's demise. It would make leaving Indiana for the peace of Manhattan that much easier—and come that much sooner.

Just a few more loose ends.

One was the announcement that Proctor Alliance was aligned to streamline all medical facilities in the great Hoosier State with its state-of-the-art security software and supply chain by the end of the following calendar year. One more year, then Indiana would finally be on the map for true innovation.

And it would be Jordan who would be praised.

If he could figure out where Craig would be when that news hit, he'd love to film his reaction and play it over and over. The blood draining. The vein in his neck bulging like it did at that groomer place yesterday. That's likely where Craig was hiding out now, as only active employees were given invites to this. And Tanberg said Mel flipped and "was out."

Certainly Craig was holed up with his mutts, licking his wounds.

He stuffed the invitation back in his jacket and felt for his speech notes. He was getting amped up, like he usually does before a presentation. Invitations. His presence alone should warrant entry; he shouldn't need an invitation.

He also shouldn't require iron-clad TSA paperwork to board a flight with his prosthetic leg, but he carried it with him every time he traveled like someone else's lackey.

For this, Jordan would forgive himself.

And lay the blame directly at the feet of the one responsible in the first place.

Dr. Craig Thompson.

38

Mel busied herself fussing with details with the hostess stand. The coat check. The table settings. She triple-checked the speaker order for the ceremony and even made her way to the kitchen to annoy the catering crew.

Everything was underway and flowing smoothly.

Just like it had flowed at the Vanderbilt building before the gunman entered. The security detail was sparse—Blane was saving money since the Proctor Alliance weapons detection software had promised it could deliver such a marvelous heads-up. It failed on that promise. Even a few meager seconds of warning would've made such a difference in so many lives.

In all of Indianapolis.

In Mel's ability to cope with herself all these months.

Moments before the shots were fired at Vanderbilt, everything was underway and flowing smoothly.

She brushed her palms down the front of her dress to steady and dry them. On muscle memory, she started the box breathing technique Dr. T. had taught her.

Dr. T.

She squared her shoulders, bucking against anything he'd put in her life. She'd been at this for days, fighting him in her head. Fighting her muscle memory go-to therapy techniques. She inhaled, exhaled, plastered a smile on her face—and turned to face the crowd.

The more people that arrived, the more anxious she should've become. She eyed every trash can and planter, even the ones deep in the venue that she knew held no security devices at all.

But then, dress blues everywhere she looked. Backs straight, heads up and alert. Weapons on hips. Dogs by their sides. Ears perked and noses on point.

Craig had come through, true to his word. Her heart rate slowed, and she reminded herself of the plan.

Tanberg. Tanberg was her plan. One she had complete control over. All the parts. It wouldn't be pretty, quite clumsy actually. But she could only do so much. These men were over the top in their cockiness and confidence. She needed help.

Help of her own choosing.

Craig could do his thing without any more involvement from her.

All she had to do was wait for the therapist to loosen up. His time spent at the bar was doing a good job of that by the looks of things. He and Eli buddying up with Scotches in sparkling glasses.

Get him talking...

Then walk out like she never had to see these people again.

Because she didn't.

39

THE GAL at the hostess stand didn't question Craig's invitation. She glanced at it and gave him a hearty welcome to the Caring Hands Banquet. She hoped he enjoyed his evening and leave "blessed beyond measure."

"Thanks."

Blessed beyond measure.

At one point that meant a long life lived with Emma. Now? Blessed looks different.

Blessed looks like seeing Toby happy and healthy. Blessed looks like forging new friendships.

Man, he was getting sappy. *Focus, Dr. Thompson.*

Blessed looks like Jordan Proctor brought up on charges.

Blessed looks like— "Mel!"

Lost in his own world, checking his pocket again, toes still frozen and totally not focused, he bumped right into her. Neither were looking. She was as startled as he was.

"Craig!"

Craig followed her scared glance over her shoulder at the bar where Tanberg was belly-laughing, and Eli was attempting to be charming with a young server. By the look on that girl's face, he was failing miserably.

"Time to get this show on the road, I guess." Craig took a step to the side of Mel, giving her a smile that he hoped communicated all was okay with the two of them despite having not spoken to her in a couple of days.

"Craig." She sidestepped with him and laid her hand on his chest, looking directly up at his face. "I've got this one. Please. I know I've not been around—" She inhaled deeply and glanced back at the bar where her two manipulators guffawed and carried on like they owned the place. She lowered her voice. "Please. I need to do this on my own."

What he saw in that second wasn't the Melody Atkins of a few weeks ago with the trembling voice and shaking hands, scared of her own shadow. She wasn't even fidgeting with her evening bag. He followed her gaze again and covered her hand with his. The woman in front of him in the flowing black dress flashed fierceness and confidence. She *belonged* here.

"Okay."

"Okay? Just like that?"

"Just like that." Craig let her hands go, and she took a step back. "Mel, I didn't tell—"

"Not now. We don't have time."

He nodded. "You need anything from me?"

"No. I have one chance. I have exactly one resource—a human one—and I've got to do this my way without rescue." She glanced down to her feet. "Without having to depend on someone else to get me out of another complicated jam."

"Okay."

She took another step away. "You'd better get after your man. Jordan Proctor, right?"

"Yeah. Mel. Be careful. These guys are—"

"Oh, I know what these guys are." She smiled at him. A bright, strong smile. "These guys are done."

40

CRAIG WALKED AWAY. His presence here both comforted Mel and threatened to unsettle her nerve, so she pushed him to the back of her mind. He headed to the grand hall where large round tables covered with crisp white linens were starting to fill. Ladies in flowing gowns, men in tuxes, first responders in full uniform. Dogs.

Mel and Riki sourced chrysanthemums and roses in reds and oranges—about the only thing Proctor Alliance didn't supply—for the centerpieces. Four huge chandeliers sparkled as a dozen members from the Indianapolis Symphony Orchestra started, bringing attention to the banquet hall. The ceremonies were about to begin.

Linda was standing near the bar. Eli was chatting up Riki now, and Tanberg was sliding his empty Scotch glass across the bar, waving off the bartender.

This was her moment.

She sent a single text and approached the bar, standing directly between Linda and the therapist.

"I know what you did."

"What?" Tanberg stood up a little straighter and tried to orient himself. "Hey, Melody. You okay, there dear?"

Mel hoped she didn't cringe outwardly at the "dear" and repeated, "I know what you did," a little louder this time. She pointed at him with her bag, hoping Linda caught the exchange. She had.

True to form, the hound dog of Human Resources never missed a trick and was nosy beyond belief. Mel sensed her stepping closer.

"You shared my file with Eli McTilde, didn't you?"

Now she had Eli's attention. And Riki's.

Witnesses. Witnesses who understood patient confidentiality better than most.

Eli joined in. "What's this about? You been drinking, Mel?"

"Not a drop. Not for a long time, isn't that right Dr. T.? We've talked about this in our sessions. How I'm to lay off the alcohol. But you already told Eli, otherwise why would he ask that?"

Not a line she'd planned, but Eli teed that baby up, and she was going to take all the swings offered her.

Bruce Tanberg held his tongue, and her pulse amped up.

Maybe I didn't wait long enough for him to loosen up. Maybe that's all he'll say.

She tried again. "You knew everything about me. Where I'd be. *When* I'd be. Manipulated me with Craig. Eli even found Craig and I at one of our dinners."

Dr. Tanberg's eyes widened. "I didn't tell him that. You didn't tell me that. You said you wanted out. I only told him about—I mean Proctor, I mean Under—"

Bingo.

Mel turned to Linda. "You heard that right? Is that

enough to have these guys looked in to? Licenses revoked, something?"

"Now listen here. I didn't know you guys would be on a date that day—" Eli tried to back-peddle. I just wanted to find Craig after he clocked me—"

"You knew where I'd be because I told *him* in my sessions. And in my texts to his personal number. You knew about my sessions and blabbed about them all over the restaurant."

"Is this the case Dr. McTilde? Dr. Tanberg?" Linda, ever the stickler for the rules, went from the matriarch of the black-tie benefit into worked-for-assholes-way-too-long in a matter of seconds.

"Got your text. How's my lady doing?" Trevor was at Mel's shoulder, winking. He was dressed in his Navy uniform and had blended in with the crowd so well she wasn't sure he'd shown up.

She smiled at him and kissed him on the cheek as Linda raged on. The doctors fairly melted in front of her, stammering out excuses and walk-backs. "She's taking them to task. May need to arrange a quiet escort out of the building."

"Anything for you, dear."

Mel stepped back and watched the show, Linda waving her arms. Trevor providing a "presence."

"Don't delete those texts. Any of them," Linda barked at her. Mel had no plans to do that. She knew this wasn't over, but for now, it was over.

"Yeah, and I'm gonna want those phones, boys." Trevor shot Mel another wink.

She motioned for Riki to join her further down the bar and opened her evening bag. She pulled out her badges and keys and laid them on the counter. "I quit."

Riki's jaw dropped, then she just nodded. "Good luck, girl."

Mel inhaled deep, fresh air for the first time in ages. Her handbag felt like it had lost a hundred pounds. She took one last look into the banquet hall. The décor. The turnout. The publicity.

She'd done good work.

A lot of it.

She can do good work somewhere else.

But never again for Blane Park—or anywhere Proctor Alliance's fingers have touched.

41

CRAIG CIRCLED the banquet hall twice, trying to pinpoint Jordan's location. And, trying and failing to mind his own business regarding Mel's mission. He caught glimpses of her. One where she shook her bag in Tanberg's face. Another with Trevor standing at her side.

Good for her.

She had it under control.

And in doing so, she effectively removed two of the four pawns from the game.

Underwood was on stage, shaking hands with benefactors from a position of height. His name would come up in whatever Mel's case had, no doubt. But the dollars secured tonight would still benefit patients, no need to ruin the whole event out of revenge.

Craig would deal with the easily bought frail ego that is Alfred another day.

Tonight was about gathering evidence for the lawyers—Clarence had that one in hand, running three simultaneous software tests, tweaking for weapons—plenty of those here tonight. Adjusting for general metals, with dog leashes, handbags, and pocketknives providing abundant samples. Even prosthetic—

Clarence.

Use your resources, Craig.

He shot off a text to the basement.

Craig: *Location on a long piece of titanium?*

Clarence: *You got it Doc. Give me one sec…*

Craig watched the message string as the three dots came and went.

Clarence: *Backstage. And if you're interested, I think I know three people with screws and one with a plate in his head.*

Craig: *Not interested. Stop snooping on body parts now.*

Of course, Jordan would be backstage, hiding behind Alfred's friendly face. And Proctor Alliance's CEO must be the "special guest speaker" listed in the brochure. He had just moments to catch him before he got on stage, and then who knows which direction he'd head or how long Craig would have to dodge folks that knew he shouldn't be there.

Craig asked one of the wait staff where the backstage room was. The kid just told him. Craig winced. Probably should train the staff better, but the kid's screw-up freed Craig from having to lie to get back there.

He gave one last glance around the dining hall. Mel truly had done a great job. He met eyes with Brian. Zoe Rigley and several other officers occupied his table. Hackett and Ava rested under the table. Brian adjusted his sling over his suit coat and motioned to join, but Craig waved him off. Brian gave him a head tilt that meant he probably wasn't going to stay put for long, but, like Mel, Craig needed to confront this demon alone.

He took long strides to reach the backstage door.

Took a long breath before turning the knob.

Blocked out all other sensory input. The chatter of the attendees. The orchestra. The glasses clinking. In a matter of seconds, Dr. Craig Thompson was ready to triage whatever was on the other side of the door.

42

"Well, well, well. I'm stunned, Dr. Thompson. Truly stunned. I thought you'd be hanging with the dogs tonight."

Craig found Jordan pacing, notecards flicking through his fingers. The man was cool. Didn't look startled to see him at all.

"Ready for your speech, I see?"

"Oh, it's a doozy. You should go out and listen. Front and center, Craig, front and center. I'll have Al make a space for you all special like. Your reaction when the news drops will be photo-worthy. I was just thinking about you." He pocketed the cards.

"Yeah, I'm not thinking you're going to be in the mood to give that speech." Craig reached into his pocket.

Pulled out the worn paper and tossed it on the coffee table into the fruit basket. It nestled between a banana bunch and oranges.

Jordan tilted his head and rolled his eyes as he reached for the paper. Craig sat on the couch and crossed his legs, trying really hard not to be cocky and not succeeding.

"I may not be able to complete the evidence circle for

the dialysis shootings. Or the Vanderbilt disaster." Craig fought to not allow his voice to waiver, so he breathed one more time. "Or bay two and Emma. But it's only a matter of time…"

Jordan opened the paper one-fourth of the way.

"But *that?*"

Another quarter open. A couple more folds, and Jordan would be faced with his crimes.

"That is another matter that takes you out of the game no matter what happens with your junk software and Proctor Alliance."

Confusion raced across Jordan's face and he fumbled the page flat and took in the contents. Then the murderer looked up at Craig, white as a ghost.

White as two ghosts. The names and photos of his victims displayed in front of him: Evan Forester and Angela Proctor. His wife and his best friend having an affair behind his back was too much for his evil ego. So Jordan took matters into his own hands on the George Washington. In the pandemonium that day, no one had bothered to look too closely. Just another unfortunate accident.

Until Jordan and the gang put all of Indianapolis at risk.

Took his Emma.

And used Mel as a pawn.

Then Craig looked.

"Hey, Jordan?"

"Your face is photo-worthy." Craig pulled out his phone and took a shot.

In a split second, the blood rushed back to Jordan's cheeks and the man was rushing toward Craig.

Craig rose and managed to put the couch between Jordan and himself before backing up. The exit door was five steps away. Jordan was two steps away and barreling around the couch. Craig took him in a bear hug, full force, and both men toppled against the press bar of the door and out into the cold night.

In the microsecond it took for Craig to get his feet under him, Jordan landed a solid jab across Craig's cheek. His skin split and the sting of the cold rushed into the cut as the blood started down his face.

Fully upright, Craig ducked the next blow. Jordan struggled to keep his footing in the snow, dress shoes not giving him any traction. Craig dropped his right shoulder and charged Jordan's chest. Both men fell, Craig knocking the air out of Jordan as they landed in the snow.

Craig was vaguely aware of light spilling onto them as they wrestled, Jordan trying to rise, spitting profanities and accusations that Craig ruined his life. Craig trying to get the guy to hold still so he could get a knee on his chest and keep him pinned.

In an instant, the air was filled with shouts and growls and fur brushing against him.

"Ava, Pass Auf, Pass Auf." Ava dropped near Jordan's head, growling and spitting, in full obedience to Officer Rigley's firm command.

Craig rose, allowing Zoe and Ava room to work. Before he could step back more than a foot or two, the door opened again and another round began.

"Hackett, no! No!" Brian was flopping at the end of Hackett's leash, and when they hit the snow cover, Brian hit his ass and let the leash go, likely saving his other shoulder from dislocation.

Free, Hackett aimed for Jordan's left foot, clamped down his jaws, and pulled while Ava held her prey in check.

The shepherd shook his prize free in a matter of seconds

and was dancing around the back lot with Jordan Proctor's prosthesis like it was a stick found at a pond.

Jordan began to sob, and Ava nudged in closer. "That dog's not allowed to do that! Stop him. I'll sue."

"Good luck with that." Brian struggled to stand and cradle his arm at the same time. "He's retired."

"Ava, fuss." Zoe, trying not to laugh, pulled her cuffs as her Malinois released the terror over Jordan and stood at her partner's side. "Good, Ava." Zoe and Craig helped Jordan onto his good leg.

"You should've done your job. I was a man. Not a useless child. A man. And you handed me off to a subpar doctor with subpar skills. You could've saved me!"

Zoe cuffed Jordan's wrists as his left pant leg blew in the wind as Hackett ran circles away from Brian with the titanium limb.

"Jordan, no one could've saved you. Then or now."

43

THE SICILIAN WAS BUZZING, busier than it had ever been since its grand opening. Craig and Rhett, mostly Rhett, pulled strings with Sadie to rent the whole back portion out for their celebration.

"We'll be bringing dogs and big tips."

"I don't know about the dogs."

"No tips and no more business." Rhett flashed her a smile, and Craig watched the waitress melt.

Sadie relented. Toby and the K-9 gang were allowed honorary station at The Sicilian as long as they wore leashes and vests. Toby looked ridiculous in a police dog vest, the lab being the furthest thing from law and order as Dianna's dumb Winston bulldog.

Even the Yorkie came, in her carrier—a police vest would have swallowed Tink. Nate and his daughter gladly accepted the invitation. "Man, Jordan stole my dog. My kid's dog!" Nate fit right in with the officers and even tolerated Clarence, who was sure he'd be the stolen Yorkie's owner should one not be found. Nate's little girl was smitten with Toby, who allowed the child to hide under the table with him and Tink and read books that Clarence pirated onto the girl's iPad for this occasion.

The door chime alerted Trevor's arrival. He brought Danishes, insisting no Italian desert could rival them. One taste and everyone agreed.

"Where'd you buy these?" Clarence took another huge bite of a raspberry one.

"Buy? Man, I don't buy these." He made the motion of whipping batter. "I hand-craft these in my own abode."

Clarence, mouth still full, gave Trevor a good attempt at a "Hooyah!"

Craig leaned back in the booth, thoroughly enjoying the mix of people. All different ages and stages. Happy. Alive. Snarky. Every one of them.

And every one of them healing from something. Their own flavors of grief.

Joel and his mom joined; Rhett and Sadie got them situated at a table. Joel presented purple flowers to Mel. "These were Emma's favorite color. She'd be proud of what you all did."

Mel smelled the blooms and thanked the boy. She sat across from Craig in the same booth as the night she'd brought him the folder. A quiet calm centered over her like he'd never seen before—even way back in high school and dreaming of their life together.

"You doin' okay?" Craig asked.

"Yeah. You?"

"I'm getting there." He fiddled with the condiment caddy and then fished out notecards from his back pocket. "Thought you'd like to see this. What you helped stop."

Mel took the cards and flipped through them. "Was this going to be his speech? Jordan's speech?" Her eyes got wider and wider the further she went.

"We did good work, Mel. And it was because of you and your attention to detail that any of it ended."

"All of Indy? Can you imagine how many more people would be at risk?"

"Legal says we've got enough to open the case again, which is all we can ask for. But Jordan's off the board."

"And down a leg." She nodded toward Hackett. Brian, lucky to have just one shoulder in a sling, shared a table with Zoe and a few other officers. Ava and Hackett rested shoulder to shoulder under the table.

"You did good with Tanberg, too. Quite the sting."

She'd told him right after how empowering it felt to finally be in control of her future. She didn't know what she wanted out of life, but she knew she wasn't going to settle and struggle like she'd done for years. Time for her to spread her wings and decide what she wants her life to look like; and now she has the confidence to do it.

"It was a human resources thing. A use-what-you've-got deal. A little sloppy, a little dicey, but it worked. And Trevor and I are tight now, yeah?" She winked over at his table, he winked back.

That was another thing Mel was right about. Human resources. Craig hoped to be a valuable resource to this gang and pay them back a hundred-fold—even if it is just shoulder reductions and nutrition counseling. Clarence's nervous system may not fire too well if he keeps pounding all those energy drinks. And Hackett was going to be the death of Brian's ligaments.

Mel was done with the notecards and passed them back to Craig. His hands wrapped around hers and they stayed that way until Sadie arrived at their table. She put down her lighter and two empty take-out boxes—even before the food arrived. "You two need to figure this out. You're giving me whiplash."

Craig moved his hands back to his side of the table and pocketed the cards as the three laughed. Sadie added, "Seriously, guys. Light the candle." She walked away with the boxes.

Mel picked up the lighter and flicked the flame on and off.

Craig's pulse quickened and he felt that nervous anxiety edging along his ribs. *Triage, Craig. Use what you know.*

Deep breath as he watched the flame dance at the end of the lighter.

Delayed: Career path. Groomer by day, trauma doc by night? He had no idea. But there was time and more space in his head to figure this one out later. Wagz would be wholly his, at any rate. Brian secured a great loan on the Bella Square storefront property, so Clarence and Craig were all set, thanks to Rivers Realty.

Urgent: Closure for Emma. He'd contacted Emma's parents after Jordan's arrest. He'd reconnected with them. They will always be part of his life, and time with them has helped to heal the grief. At least part of it.

Immediate? Craig held Mel's gaze. She smiled and raised an eyebrow at him, still flicking the lighter. He smiled back.

Immediate: Secure the lighter. Check.

Light the candle. Check.

Let the fresh start begin...

ABOUT THE AUTHOR

Beth enjoys chucking words into sentences then standing back to see what magic—or mayhem—falls out, crafting tales in mystery, sci-fi, fantasy, and general "slice of life" fiction. She couldn't accomplish this without the help of her tutu-clad Little Miss Muse and Trudi the Concrete Office Goose, who's partial to superhero capes.

Her stories have appeared in multiple publications, including Pulphouse Fiction Magazine and Ellery Queen Mystery Magazine, and in multiple fiction anthologies. She's received several Honorable Mentions from Writers of the Future. Her lighthearted blog peeks into the writing life as she pokes fun at herself and her circus of a life.

Follow the antics of Little Miss Muse and Trudi, read Beth's blog (she might have burned down her kitchen last week), and discover the stories at bapaul.com.

Short Story Collections

Spunk and Spice, Volumes 1 and 2: A Collection of six short stories celebrating timeless wit and wisdom.

Out There, Volumes 1 and 2: A Collection of six short sci-fi and speculative tales.

Mystery Minutes, Volumes 1 and 2: Six short mystery stories

All the Feels, Volumes 1, 2, and 3: Collections of inspiring short stories

Just a Tick of Whimsy, Volumes 1 and 2: Collections of fantasy shorts.

Hijacked Holidays: Definitely not your warm-and-fuzzy winter tales.

Dark Minds: Toe-curling twisted mysteries.

Blog Compilations: Slices of the writing life with lots of laughs and bumps in the road.

Life Along the Way

Life All Over Again

Young Adult (or Young at Heart) Books

Switch: Book 1 in the Oliver Andrews Trilogy

STAY IN TOUCH!

BAPAUL.COM

Take a glimpse into B.A. Paul's writing journey, including the ups and downs of managing family, "real jobs," ducks in wobbling rows, and chasing down her Little Miss Muse. New blog posts go up Mondays, with the first Monday of the month reserved for a free fiction short story available on the blog for a limited time.

Newsletter Signup!
Get the latest release information, author updates, and exclusive content by signing up with your email at bapaul.com.

www.ingramcontent.com/pod-product-compliance
Lightning Source LLC
Chambersburg PA
CBHW060445310726

48977CB00001B/324